30 DAYS OF
SHAME

GINGER TALBOT

Thirty Days of Shame

PROLOGUE

A rural area of the Pevlova Oblast, several hours east of the Leningrad Oblast, in Russia
June 2017

The countryside is a lush oil painting come to life, too beautiful to be real. A warm breeze ruffles the oak leaves, and the sunlight filters through the dense tree canopy, bathing the ground in syrupy golden light. The soft moss swallows the sound of footsteps.

Not everyone can appreciate the day's beauty, however.

The cargo has been unloaded. The cargo is crying. It doesn't matter. The area is thickly wooded, and there are no other houses for miles. No one to hear their screams, their pleas. They're about to be hustled into the basement of a crumbling farmhouse, to await the auction tomorrow night.

Cataha has been waiting for the cargo for an hour. Impatience chews at him as he walks over to the miserable, weeping crowd of women, huddled together on the weed-choked driveway.

A man with yellow teeth and breath that stinks of onions grins and waves at the cargo. "They're ready for your inspection, Mr. – sorry – Cataha."

Cataha gives the man, Ygor, a look that threatens death if he makes that mistake again. The man knows his real name from past dealings with him, but nobody speaks his real name here. He has chosen a new name – the Russian word for Satan – to separate himself from his past with one clean and vicious slice.

"Mr. who?" His hand drifts to the Stechkin automatic pistol he has holstered on his right hip.

"Sorry, sir." Ygor swallows hard and looks at the ground.

Once upon a time, Cataha would have killed the man for such a slip-up. Slashed his throat right there, as an example to the others. He doesn't need weak, stupid dullards working for him. Now, with his forces and finances severely depleted, he is forced to tolerate fools. But not forever. And he has a very long memory.

He turns to survey the delivery, and his anger recedes a little. A cruel smile curls his lips.

Twenty women.

Beautiful. Young. Terrified.

The heavenly trifecta.

There are four men guarding them, including Ygor, and one man stationed a mile down the weed-choked dirt side-road. He would like to have triple that number, but he simply couldn't afford it.

He used to swim in a sea of rubles, sable and pussy. His mansion could swallow a small town. Now he's living under a fake name, in hiding, cutting corners everywhere. Hatred gnaws at his gut, and he imagines his enemies strapped down on a table in a room full of sharp instruments. Just like the old days.

The sale of this shipment will help him get back on his feet again. And the inspection is his favorite part. The sheer terror that twists their faces, the beautiful symphony of their sobs…it sends a rush of

4

blood to the groin.

Their hands are tied behind their backs, and their feet are shackled together so they can only shuffle, not run. Their clothing is stained, and they reek of fear and sweat and urine.

That's all right. They'll be bathed and stripped for the auction tomorrow night. Then they'll each have their hands attached to cuffs on chains that dangle from the ceiling, and their shiny, clean bodies will be pawed and prodded by the horde of prospective buyers.

He'd love to sample the merchandise, but they're worth more unsullied. Much more. And he needs the funds.

He can play with them a little, though. As long as their hymens are intact, they still command a virgin price. Tonight will be delightful.

He walks up and down the rows of women, his gaze cold, fingering the small whip he carries on a hook on the left side of his belt. They see the whip and cry harder. That's the point.

He strides up to one of the prettiest ones. She has thick, shiny hair the color of sun-ripened wheat, hanging halfway down her back. Full hips. Her eyes are a pale blue. Her pink lips are plump. He wants to bite them until they bleed. He wants to splatter her pale flesh with cuts and bruises. He wants to feel the snap of bone beneath his fist.

He slaps her on the side of the head. Best to establish his authority right away.

"Get on your knees, whore."

She glares at him sullenly. He hits her harder, and she staggers but still refuses to kneel for him.

He sees no fear in her gaze. Only contempt. That infuriates him.

Once everyone knew his name, and trembled when they heard it. Now this stupid peasant slut thinks she can defy him and continue to breathe.

"You want to play this game, bitch?" he roars at her.

Without warning, he reaches between her legs and squeezes hard. She screams in pain and staggers back, bumping into one of the other girls.

He moves forward and keeps squeezing, and grabs her by the hair so she can't get away from him. She is frantic, writhing, as he crushes her sex with a vise-like grip. His men rush over to watch, their eyes alight.

"Did your parents keep you pure?" he demands.

She keeps squirming, tears of pain welling in her eyes, but refuses to speak.

He already knows the answer, because these women were referred to him by a doctor on his payroll.

The women are young, disease-free virgins, from very poor families. That is important, because they will be ignored when they report their daughters missing.

The women came to a town where they believed they'd be working at a factory. They all had to submit to a medical exam when they arrived. Then all the women recommended by the doctor – the prettiest ones, who still had their hymens – were shuffled off to a separate dormitory. Last night, they were rounded up at gunpoint and hustled into a truck. The uglier women had no idea how lucky they were.

He glances at the other women, who are cringing and crying. This blonde bitch is setting a bad example. He can't let them get the idea that they can defy him. He needs them terrified. Compliant.

It's worth sacrificing one to frighten the others into submission. It will make the others more appealing to the buyers.

And it will be so much fun.

He twists his hand in her hair until she screams in pain, tears streaming down her flushed cheeks. "You know what happens to women who try to give me crap? Let me show you, while your friends watch. I know you're a virgin. And your first fuck is going to be your last, because right after I take you, I'm going to end you." He starts to drag her away from the group so he can throw her down on the ground and stab her tender hymen with his dick.

And still she refuses to beg, or even speak. She'll be begging soon enough, when he knocks her teeth down her throat and she's choking on her own blood. He's stiff just picturing it.

Today is a good day.

Except it isn't.

One of his men is on his walkie talkie, and his expression is panicked. He must be talking to the lookout.

"What is it?" Cataha yells angrily.

"The police are coming!" the man shouts back.

All four of them run for their truck, leaving him behind with the women.

"What the fuck?" he roars.

Fury chokes him. Not again. Not again!

The local cops have all been bribed. This must be Politsiya. Federal police. How? How do they keep finding his operation?

It's that journalist, the one who writes for Reforma. Somehow, the wretched bastard keeps tipping off the police. Cataha has been shut down repeatedly this year. Brothels raided, women rescued and blabbing, his men arrested. Every time he starts to get ahead, he's knocked back down again.

Screaming with rage, he pulls out his gun and points it at the defiant blonde whore's stomach. Just as he pulls the trigger, someone strikes him on the head from behind with what feels like a rock, so hard that he jerks the gun and misses the spine and vital organs, just catching the side of the blonde's midriff. The rest of the bullets spray uselessly into the grass.

The blonde goes down with a cry of pain, doubling over and

wailing.

The woman behind him bashes him twice more with the rock, shrieking like an Amazon. His head is exploding with pain and the pistol falls from his hand into the dirt. He falls to his knees and scrabbles after it, and the vile bitch kicks it hard, sending it flying into the underbrush. She's as strong as hell. Stupid peasant bitch. Then she kicks him in the head with all her might, and he vomits into the dirt.

Her hands were free, her feet were free…

So his useless men did such a shit job tying up the women that at least one of them was able to get free to grab that rock. He needs his fucking gun! He would have mowed down every last one of those bitches and made sure they didn't talk, but now he'll be lucky if he escapes with his freedom.

When he finds his men, he will open them up with a dull knife and unspool their intestines inch by inch.

He can hear sirens now.

He wants to kill every single woman there, but he has no time for revenge. He doesn't even have time to go after the pistol. He runs for his car, vomiting uncontrollably, blood streaming down the back of his head.

He flees, knowing that the disrespectful bitch he shot probably won't even die. The thought infuriates him. He hopes that someday he'll be able to track her down and finish the job.

But now, even as he's tearing down the road, tires spewing up clouds of dirt, he's planning how to deal with that journalist. He's just lost a huge amount of money, and the good will of his prospective buyers. He can't risk pulling together another shipment until he knows he's plugged the leaks.

Cataha will live up to his name. He'll drag that reporter straight to hell.

ONE

Day zero...

Columbus, Ohio, July 2017

It's 10:30 a.m. and I stifle a yawn as I head to my lunch shift at the Cuppa Joe diner. I've already been awake for five hours.

My aunt and my cousins were still sleeping when I woke up and spent two hours on the dark web, visiting websites that teach me how to hack, then practicing my newly acquired skills. I do that every day. I'm trying to find the answer to an urgent question. What is Operation Salvat?

When I finished websurfing at 7:30 a.m., I woke up my aunt Anastasia and my cousins Helenka and Yuri.

After a quick breakfast, we peeked through the curtains of our apartment before we left, scanning for anyone or anything that didn't belong there. Only when we were sure that we were clear did we leave the apartment.

Of course, we checked around us continuously as we walked to the private gym where we get free self-defense lessons, courtesy of a local women's group. And we did the same when we walked back to the apartment building.

We've only been training for a couple of months now, ever since we went on the run from Sergei, and I wouldn't say we're ninja-level, or even badass-level, or, okay, the least bit scary. But we've learned some cool tricks that would at least give us a chance if Sergei or my Uncle Vilyat or any of the other shady figures from our past came after us.

I relax a little as I approach the diner. The sidewalks are crowded in the downtown district during the day. Crowds are anonymous. They swallow me up and I'm just one cell in a multi-celled organism. Invisible, indistinguishable.

Cuppa Joe has a green awning and a big plate glass window that turns into a bright mirror during the day. It's a movie screen reflecting back the comfortingly dull daily rituals of downtown life. Right now, like clockwork, office buildings spit out streams of cubicle drones on their lunch break, and they flow towards the strip of road where all the restaurants huddle together.

I stare at the mirror-window as I stride up, looking for my reflection. As usual, it takes a couple of seconds before I can pick myself out of the crowd.

But then, I'm not really me anymore.

Three months ago, at the beginning of April, I was shoved into the back of Sergei Volkov's limousine. He changed me, broke me, leaving me to put myself back together again. Broken things are never the same after you glue them back together, though. I am reinvented and made new, from the inside out.

Now I wear glasses, although I have perfect vision and the plastic lenses are clear. I slashed my long dishwater-blonde hair into a chin-length wavy bob and dyed it brown. I used to wear very little makeup; here I paint and cake it on. Red lipstick, rosy blush, cat-eye eyeliner. Anything to blur the resemblance of my new self, Sarah Maynard, to my old self, Willow Toporov.

They say change is good. But this is disguise, not change. My aunt, my cousins, me…we're not much freer now than we were back in California, living under my Uncle Vilyat's suffocating, abusive regime. Every decision we make, from what we look like to our daily schedule, is calculated to erase our old selves.

Then again, Aunt Anastasia is no longer having her bones broken and her face tenderized by the man who swore to love, honor and cherish her. Nine-year-old Yuri has stopped flinching every time someone raises their voice or makes a sudden movement. Thirteen-year-old Helenka won't be married off to a gross old mob boss for political advantage in a few years.

I'm not sure why I'm in such a dark mood right now. Everything is going well. Two months ago, a sympathetic hotel clerk gave us a few hundred bucks of her hard-earned money so we could make it all the way to Columbus. Since then, I've managed to find passable fake identification for my aunt and cousins, and the kids can start school in September. Anastasia's been weaned off prescription drugs, and she's on the computer all day long taking online classes. She's working towards a certificate in computer security. She and I have hacking contests sometimes. She's at least as good as me.

There hasn't been a single sign of trouble, but I realize as I walk into Cuppa Joe that I'm unusually jumpy today.

The familiar din pounds my ears, a mixture of conversation and music pumping from the jukebox.

I stand by the door and do a quick visual sweep of the room. Nothing jumps out at me.

Why is the hair standing up on the back of my neck?

There's already a decent mid-morning crowd as I punch my timecard and go into the kitchen to memorize the day's specials. I scan the customers again through the window; lots of regulars, nothing seems out of place.

But I remember what one of our self-defense instructors tells us all the time. Trust your gut.

My gut is tying itself in knots.

I'm still a few minutes early. I duck into the break room, head to my locker, and grab my apron and order pad.

After I've tied on my apron and stuffed my pad and pens in the pockets, as well as some bills and quarters so I can make change, I call my aunt.

"Is everything all right?" I ask her.

"Of course." Her voice is wary. "Why wouldn't it be? Has something happened?"

I don't want to freak her out, but I want her to be on the lookout for...I don't know what.

"I don't know. I just have a weird feeling. Can you make sure that Helenka and Yuri are okay?"

"Sure."

A minute goes by. I hear her walking around the apartment, and then her voice is back, panicked. "Helenka is gone."

Fear blossoms inside me, and the stuffy room suddenly feels like a suffocating trap.

Think. Don't panic. Panicking never solved anything.

"What about the alarm?" I demand. We have an alarm system with sensors on every door, every window.

"Hold on, hold on..." I hear her hurrying down the hallway. "It's still enabled. Someone entered Helenka's code five minutes ago. I was in the shower; I didn't hear. And Yuri was playing a video game with the headphones on."

That is against protocol. If she was in the shower, both Yuri and Helenka should have been on the alert, in case someone started kicking in a door or window.

Where is Helenka right now? Is she being raped? Cut to pieces?

"Damn it, Anastasia, how many times do we have to go over this?" I snap. "We are never safe. We can never relax."

I can hear Yuri crying in the background. He comes right up to the phone. "I'm sorry, I'm sorry! It's all my fault!"

Once upon a time, his loving, supportive cousin Willow Toporov would have comforted him. But now I'm Sarah Maynard, and Sarah is a mean, paranoid bitch focused on survival, not hugs and kisses.

"Yes, it is your fault, you and your mother, because you know what to do and you chose not to! Check her cell phone location. I'll do the same."

We all have cell phones with tracking enabled on them.

"I'll hang up and call you back." Anastasia's voice is rising in terror. She's about to completely lose it. If I were there, I'd slap her so hard her ears would ring. We don't have the luxury of getting hysterical. After all our training for every possible emergency, this is how easily she falls apart?

We both hang up. My hands are shaking as I stab the screen on the phone with my fingers. I am desperately searching for the "find my phone" app. Damn it, I'm no better than Anastasia. Our first real emergency, and I'm losing it too. Tears burn in my eyes, and I blink frantically. It takes me three tries to get the app working.

Please don't be dead, please don't be dead…

I enter Helenka's location into the cell phone, and at the same time, my phone rings. Helenka is calling me.

Relief flows over me like a tidal wave, quickly followed by a prickly red anger.

"What the hell?" I snap into the phone.

"I just went to get the mail," Helenka says miserably. "I just wanted to get out of the house for a minute. I had my phone with me the whole time. I checked around me. I practiced my situational awareness."

"You are not allowed to leave the house without your mother, and you know that. You left without even telling her or Yuri? You both screwed up, big time. Why don't you just hang a big 'kidnap me' sign around your neck if you're so eager to be taken?"

"I am not eager to be taken." Now she's crying.

"Then act like you want to live another day. We will discuss this when I get home." My heart rate starts to slow back down again.

"I hate that our life is like this! I hate it, Willow!" she sobs.

I stifle a groan. "Helenka, I hate it too. But we know what our choices are. We live like this, or you go back to your father, and he locks you away for a few years, then marries you off to some fat old pig for a lifetime of misery. And if he catches your mother, he'll kill her. And beat Yuri senseless. Those are our choices. We hide, or we get caught and our life is a living hell. Are we clear?"

"Yes. We're clear." Her voice is sad and resigned, and it cuts into me. Helenka is lonely and bored and isolated, and I just ripped her to shreds for wanting the tiniest bit of freedom.

I hang up before I give in to my impulse to apologize to her. She can't think it's okay to let down her barriers, ever, not even for a single second.

I head into the restaurant and start taking orders.

An hour goes by in a blur. I'm so rattled that I'm checking out everyone and everything, looking at them through the dark lens of suspicion.

I recognize a handsome guy who's been in before. Phillip. A lawyer. He's wearing a nice suit, and he smells good. He smiles at me with perfect white teeth.

"Say…Sarah, is it?"

"Yes."

"I was just wondering, do you ever have any free time after work?"

I instantly go into what I call "polite retreat" mode. "That is very sweet of you, but I've got a boyfriend."

Disappointment crinkles around his eyes, and he nods, sounding a little sad. "He's a lucky man."

I hurry off to take orders from another table. Maybe he was genuinely a nice guy. Maybe he could have been 'the one'.

Then again, I doubt it. Being with Sergei did things to me.

When he was being a bastard, he was the meanest, most loathsome son of a bitch I've ever met. And I grew up in a family of mobsters. But when he touched me...the sex was something I've never experienced before. Terrifying and exhilarating, like the swoop of a roller coaster ride. Insanely orgasmic. I still crave it, with a hunger that can never be slaked. I can't imagine another man's hands on me.

Unfortunately, Sergei is a stone-cold psychopath. Not only that, I broke an agreement that I'd made with him; I was supposed to stay with him for thirty days, and I left on the twenty-seventh. When I tried to go back, he threatened me.

Even if I wanted to go back, I couldn't. Not that it matters; I don't want to go back – I think.

Sergei has split me in two. My brain tells me I never want to see him again, but my body wants to fly back into his arms. I feel like a junkie going through withdrawal; when I lie in bed, I literally ache for him. He's my beautiful, savage fever dream, he's a phantom who haunts my waking and sleeping moments.

Unwelcome images flash through my brain as I move from one table to the next on autopilot.

Me, tied down, legs spread wide, vulnerable and exposed. Sergei's tongue stroking me until I'm weeping and begging for release. His hard hand smacking on my ass while his finger strokes the tiny pink pearl between my legs. I force the thoughts from my head; they make me ache with longing, and it disgusts me. Why don't I have more self-respect? Why does my heart pound faster for a man who insulted and rejected me?

As I'm heading to the cook's window to put in my orders, the day manager, Harold, comes over to me. He's short and fat and always has an apologetic look on his face when he asks for anything. He's about as scary as a teddy bear with the stuffing leaking out, but in my heightened state of paranoia, I feel like he looks shifty and out of sorts.

"Hey, Sarah, how you doing today?"

I smile and nod my head, like one of those bobblehead toys that people put on their dashboards. "Just great, thanks."

"Do you mind taking out the trash?"

I frown in puzzlement. Odd request. That's the busboy's job, and it's really busy right now. "I've got to put in two orders."

He snatches my order pad from my hand. "I'll do it. Please take out the trash."

I see his eyes shuttle to the side, and I know. Damn it. I'm not being paranoid; I'm right.

Somebody's gotten to him.

My heart pounds faster.

I refuse to budge. "Why aren't you asking the busboy to do it?"

A frown creases Harold's forehead. He huffs out an exasperated sigh. "He's busy."

I glance at the busboy. He's flirting with one of the waitresses. "No he isn't."

"Look, do your job or get fired." His voice is unnaturally high. And he never speaks to me like this.

Anger floods through me. He's trying to send me out into the back alley; I can just imagine what fun things are waiting for me.

We were safe. We were just starting to rebuild our lives. Why the hell can't people just leave us alone?

"How much?" I snapped.

His eyes widen, and he takes a step back.

I move towards him. "How much money did it cost to sell me out, asshole?" I grind the words out. I'm taking off my apron as we speak. My job is done here. I'm unemployed, just like that.

He takes another step backwards, eyes like saucers. I've backed him against a wall. "I don't know what you're talking about!"

I keep staring at him, and he goes pale. He's almost crying. "Please. He said he'd cut up my wife and baby girl. He knows their names. He knows where we live."

Now would that be Sergei, or my uncle Vilyat, or my Uncle Edik? Because it could be literally anyone from my former social circle.

How messed up is my life?

I head for the front door. I pull my cell phone out of my pocket and Harold tries to grab it from me.

"Get your hands off me!" I shriek at the top of my lungs. The din dies down. People are staring at us.

"Get back here! You…you stole my phone!" he tries to bluster.

"This phone?" I wave it over my head. It's pink and has flowers on it.

He gives up and hurries towards the back door.

I quickly dial Anastasia.

"We're burned," I say. "I don't know who it is. Grab your go-bags. You guys meet me at the location, you know when. Remember plan B. And if I don't show, you run, and you keep running." I don't say specifics in case somehow someone has hacked into our phones.

We also have a plan C, D, E… I drill our plans into their skulls every night.

"Willow! No!" Anastasia cries. "We won't leave without you."

"I did all of this for you and the kids," I insist. "Especially the kids. As long as you guys are safe, everything will be all right. If you're taken, this was all for nothing."

"I can't do this myself." Her voice is shaking with terror. Anastasia's never been a strong woman. She's nine years older than me, but I'm the one who runs the show, the one who makes all the decisions. I've tried to get her to be more independent, but every time I insist that she make a decision about anything, she has panic attacks and her chest starts heaving, and it freaks out the kids.

"Fucking man up, Anastasia. You will pack up and run for it, unless you want Helenka to be married to a sixty-year-old who will pump her full of babies," I snap. "Unless you want Vilyat to beat your son until he breaks him."

I'm playing dirty pool.

That's what I am now. Dirty.

She's crying as I hang up.

I elbow my way through a crowd of customers lining up to be seated, and make it out of the front door. I step out into the bright, hot daylight, and there he is. His eyes are trained on me like lasers, powered by hate and vengeance.

This is bad. This is worse than bad. "Hello," I say, my voice steady, as my insides turn to water. Run, Anastasia, run. And never look back. "Have you come to kill me?"

TWO

The world seems to swim and shimmer in front of me, in a haze of terror.

The man before me is not who I expected.

He's the worst of all possibilities. He's an outcome I hadn't even considered.

It's Feodyr, who used to be Sergei's right-hand man, until he betrayed Sergei.

Feodyr looks even worse than the last time I saw him – the night Sergei pounded his face in.

His hair, once clipped close to his skull, is growing out, stringy and greasy. His nose is skewed to the right, and the left side of his face sags a little, forcing his lip into a permanent sneer. Nerve damage from the beating, I'd imagine. And I can actually see a dent in his skull; that's how hard Sergei punches.

When I was being held prisoner in Sergei's mansion by the sea, Feodyr was clean and immaculately dressed. He did seem to drink a lot, but he handled it just fine. Not anymore. From the looks of him, and the smell, he's been drinking non-stop since he evaded his police guard and fled the hospital a couple of months ago. That and sleeping rough. He moves in a sour fog of body odor, whiskey fumes, and reeking breath, his T-shirt and jeans are stained, and his face is puffy.

And he's carrying a newspaper...which is wrapped around the pistol that he's pointing at my stomach.

People are streaming around us on the sidewalk, talking on their phones, talking to each other. They brush by him; they're inches away from a tightly coiled bundle of rage shaped like a human. Nobody but me notices the gun.

"What are you doing here?" I ask him.

The right half his mouth twitches up a hideous mockery of a grin. "Sergei sent me. He wants me to rape, torture and murder you. Personally, I couldn't get it up for an ugly whore like you, Willow, so you'll have to settle for just the torture and murder part. I hope you aren't too disappointed."

"No he didn't," I say, keeping my voice and my expression calm. "First of all, if he wanted that done, he'd do it himself. And more importantly, there's no way you're still working for him. Looking like that? Smelling like that? He's a professional. He only hires professionals. You look like you should be in line at a soup kitchen."

Rage twists his bloated face. "You *little cunt!*"

He storms towards me. I quickly back up, into an iron railing. He moves so he's standing two feet away from me. I force myself not to look down at the gun that's ready to punch holes in my flesh.

"We're surrounded by people, in the middle of the day," I point out to him. "You think I'm just going to let you kidnap me?"

"Yes, I do, actually." He glances at a playground across the street, where mothers are pushing toddlers on swings. My heart stutters in my chest. Is he threatening to do what I think he is?

His furious gaze lights on me again. "You're right that Sergei won't let me work for him anymore. He'd kill me if he saw me. Because of you." He chokes on a sob. Sergei was everything to him. Sergei and his gang of fanatical followers, and the campaign of revenge against my family. It was all Feodyr lived for. "You ruined him. I tried to save him from you, but he was too far gone."

He thought Sergei was falling for me, to the point where he might falter in their mission. He thought wrong. But he was so afraid of Sergei developing any chink in his armor that he tried to "save" Sergei by getting rid of me. He kidnapped me and took me to a party where a gang of mobster scum were molesting women who were victims of human trafficking.

When Sergei and his men came to rescue me, they killed every last one of the mobsters and freed the women. I knew how close Sergei had been to Feodyr, so I stopped him from beating the bastard to death with his bare hands. I told him to leave Feodyr to the cops, to let him rot in prison. That was a mistake.

A mistake that will cost me my life. I probably have only hours to live, and those hours will be a nightmare.

And he's going to kill me for nothing. I didn't affect Sergei in the slightest. If I had, he wouldn't have refused me when I begged to go back.

I meet Feodyr's crazed, bloodshot gaze. "You're wrong. Sergei never cared about me. He'd have to be capable of normal human emotion to do that, and he's not. He's a psychopath. He's just better at being a psychopath than you are."

Rage twists Feodyr's features. "Shut the hell up, you..." He rattles off a stream of Russian words that I assume are an exceptionally colorful way to tell me I'm a whore. My Russian is decent, but not great, and I only know the basic swear-words.

It's ironic. Feodyr can't stand me saying a single bad thing about Sergei, even though Sergei tried to kill him.

Feodyr's face is flushing an ugly red. Sweat beads on his forehead and runs down the sides of his face. Can I reason with him? Is there any hope for me?

"I asked him if I could go back to him, and he said no!" There's an edge of pleading to my voice. "He doesn't care if I live or die! If you hurt me, he won't blink an eye. I'm nothing to him."

"You going to go down on your knees and beg?" Feodyr sneers. "Offer to suck my cock if I just let you live?"

Never.

"If you shoot me, you will be hunted down by the police and killed," I say. My heart is beating a mile a minute.

He barks out a hideous sound that I think might be a laugh. "You think I fucking care about that? About anything? This is the end for me. Today."

My heart sinks, and tears of panic prick my eyes. He's here on a suicide mission. There's no reasoning, no begging, no hope. He's staggered far, far away from the land of the sane and the rational. He's in a place where reality can't reach him.

He's swaying, and a few people glance at him because he's raised his voice, but nobody stops to help me. I can't say I blame them; Feodyr is big and scary-looking, and menace rolls off him like a stinking toxic fog.

He glances at the playground again. Then his gaze returns to me. He shakes the gun, and the newspaper rattles. "You can come with me right now, or I will shoot the children in the playground, and then shoot you in the gut. Either way you'll die in agony, but if you stay here, you'll be taking a bunch of innocent children with you." He grimaces. I think he's trying to sneer at me.

I want to scream with frustration. Because I was born into the wrong family, my only life choices are to pick a horrible nightmare scenario, or an even worse nightmare scenario.

It would be *my* fault if Feodyr murdered a bunch of preschoolers? It was *my* fault that Sergei held me as collateral for my uncle's five-million-dollar debt, and treated me like a slave because of crimes that my family committed against him?

But trying to point that out to him would be a waste of breath – and I know I don't have many breaths left.

"Fine," I spit. "I'll go with you."

"Drop your cell phone on the ground."

I obey him, pulling the cell phone from my pocket and dropping it.

It's okay. Anastasia and the kids are safe. That's all that matters.

But I don't want to die. I don't, I don't, I don't.

I let him lead me around a corner, down an alleyway, and to a parking lot. He drags me over to a car. The parking lot attendant is sitting in the booth, ignoring us so hard that I know that Feodyr paid him off. He glances around, then pops open the trunk.

My breakfast rises in my throat. Tears blur my vision. This is the end. If I run and scream, he'll kill other people, then kill me anyway.

The last decent thing I can do with my life is save a bunch of strangers who will never know what I did for them.

I can't help myself. I let out a single, hiccuping sob. I hate myself for it, because I hear Feodyr snicker in response.

Helenka. Yuri. Anastasia. I am sorry. I am so, so sorry to leave you.

He spins me around, quickly binds my hand behind me with a zip tie, and scoops me up in his arms. I try not to retch at his stinking body. He drops me into the trunk with a rough thud.

"Make any noise, try to draw any attention to yourself, and I'll shoot you," he says. He slams the trunk shut, and instantly I'm swallowed up in suffocating darkness. A sense of claustrophobia strangles me, and I struggle not to scream as the car starts moving.

It's hot, and sweat beads on my forehead as the car jolts and races down the road. I think of my family. I think of Lukas, the little boy Sergei is caring for. Lukas is being raised by an elderly couple, and he is so sad, so lonely for his mother, that he took one look at me and decided that I was her. He thought I was his mother, come back for him, and he latched on to me like a barnacle.

That child loved me. I've thought about him every single day since the day I left. I had planned on trying to find a way to contact him, to let him know that I didn't want to leave him. Unless I can get out of this trunk, he'll grow up and grow old and die thinking I abandoned him.

I try to pay attention to where we're going. I think we're moving away from downtown.

Questions race through my mind.

How the hell did he find me? I'm using fake ID, a fake social security number. I don't look anything like I used to. I haven't gotten in touch with anyone back home. Not only that, but he has to have been living life on the run. He can't have just strolled into an internet café or a library with Wi-Fi and found me by searching online.

Sergei has endless resources. Feodyr no longer has any access to them.

If I survive this, I will need to figure out what mistake I made that exposed me like this.

But right now, I have to move fast.

I've been preparing for something like this for the last two months. Being kidnapped and thrown into the trunk of a car is terrifying, but it is also on the list of scenarios I've prepared for. If he'd been smart, he'd have pulled my shoes off.

But he didn't. And now I'm going to find out if all my practice has paid off. It was so easy when I did it in our apartment, again and again. Now my hands are shaking and sweaty, and I'm so crazed with fear that I can barely think straight.

I curl my legs up behind me and dig the small blade out of the inside of my shoe, where I taped it. Awkwardly, I rub it against the zip tie and strain until the tie snaps.

Yes! A tiny victory!

Then I scrabble around in the trunk for the release latch, and fumble with it until I get the lid open. I don't let it open all the way, though; I don't want Feodyr to glance in the rearview mirror and see that the trunk is open until the time is right. Falling out into traffic and dying under the wheels of a speeding car isn't my goal.

I wait until I feel the car slow to a stop, idling. I think we're at a stop sign. I know we're further away from downtown now. Less chance of collateral damage.

I pop the trunk wide open and roll out into the street. I've calculated correctly; we're idling next to a park. I run for my life.

I hear Feodyr's howls of rage tearing through the air, and then the *pop pop pop* of gunfire as I dodge behind a tree and bend low to run behind a row of hedges.

Seek cover. Be a moving target. Harder to hit.

And miracle of miracles, two police officers are on bicycle patrol in the park, and they spot him.

Feodyr starts shooting at them. People scream and scatter, dropping briefcases and lunch boxes and paper cups of coffee.

The police fire back at him.

I run and run, and a cramp burns my side, and I stagger but make my legs keep moving. When the gunfire stops, I pause to glance back. Feodyr is prone on the ground, curled up on his side. Both cops are alive. People are crouching behind trees, behind garbage cans, hugging each other, crying.

Almost weeping with relief, I jog away, heading down a side street.

Feodyr was too sloppy to search me. I have a second phone, and a thousand dollars cash, hidden in a bag strapped to my thigh.

I start walking towards a small, no-name motel twenty blocks from the park. I've scouted out dozens of them over the last couple of months.

Anastasia and the kids will be headed out of town right now. I don't know where they're going; we arranged that on purpose, in case someone tries to torture the information out of me.

I really want to go back to the apartment to get my laptop and pack some clothing, but I don't dare. What if Feodyr was more organized than he seemed, and has someone waiting for me?

So instead I book a room at the motel. I even manage to get the clerk to give me a room without giving them ID; it costs me an extra hundred bucks.

I lock the door, sit down on the bed, and cry, rubbing my wrists where the zip ties cut into them.

Then I call Anastasia.

"It was Feodyr," I tell her. "He's dead now. But we're still leaving town. Follow the plan. I'll check in with you at six a.m. tomorrow. If you don't hear from me, you go on your own."

I hang up on her desperate protests.

THREE

Day one...

I wake up with a jerk. I am curled on my side on a lumpy mattress under a stiff blanket, and it takes me a minute to remember where I am, and why. My brain is dull and fuzzy. I tossed and turned all night. I don't even remember falling asleep.

I'm about to sit up, but a cold wave of fear rolls over me, and I lie still. I don't know why. I listen carefully. All I hear are traffic sounds outside the room. Still, I'm afraid to move. I sense something in the room with me. If I don't move a muscle, will it go away? Or will it come closer?

I'll count to a thousand and then get up.

One, two, three, four, five, six…

"How long are you going to pretend to be asleep?" an impatient voice growls at me. "I don't have all day." I start and fall out of bed, flailing. I scramble to my feet.

Sergei. Standing there. Staring at me with an amused curl to his cruel, beautiful mouth. He's wearing a bespoke suit of light linen, and a silk shirt, in complementary tones of blue steel.

I'd forgotten how large he was – not just his body, but his presence. He's easily 6'3" and has the shoulders of a linebacker. It's that sense of animal menace prowling just under the surface that really defines him, though. When he's in a room, he's in command of everything, down to the molecules of oxygen.

He's still every bit as stunning as I remember, a beautiful savage. Cruel, sensual lips, strong, broad jaw, laser-sharp blue eyes that can pierce every defense and every lie. Something's a little different, though. I think I see shadows under his eyes, and a hollowness in his gaze.

"Hello," I choke out, absurdly. What else is there to say?

How did he find me here?

I have my burner phone…could he have used that to track me? No, not that. When I'm not using it, I keep it turned off and have the battery removed so that there's no chance anyone could use it to find me.

He smiles at me, but only with his mouth. He's standing there staring at me, a calculating glint in his gaze. The shade of his blue eyes changes depending on his mood. Today they are so icy that I feel the chill everywhere his glance brushes against me.

I cross my arms over my chest, feeling self-conscious. My hair is tangled and I'm wearing my jeans and T-shirt from yesterday.

He takes one step forward. Only one. Sergei is a monster who likes to draw out his punishments, extracting maximum terror from every single second. I force myself not to flinch or cry out.

"Willow. What's a nice girl like you doing in a place like this?" His rich, strong voice caresses my ears. It's spiced by his Russian accent, exotic and sexy and dangerous.

"I'm not that nice anymore. Thanks to you," I say.

"Oh, you'll always be a good girl, deep inside. Just because you

28

like me to do dirty things to you doesn't mean you're not a sweet, sweet woman." His voice is mocking, his gaze harsh. To him, being a decent, caring human being is a weakness.

I take a deep, shaky breath. "It can't be a coincidence that you and Feodyr showed up here at the same time."

Disgust curls his mouth. "No. I found you, and then Feodyr kidnapped one of my men and made him talk. I've been monitoring the police radio. I know he's dead now. I wish I'd been the one to end him, but the result is the same. He'll never hurt you again."

The frustration that's been bubbling up inside me explodes. I was so careful! We all were! And it was all for nothing.

"How the hell did you find me?" I demand. "Tell me!"

He moves towards me faster than thought, so fast I don't even see it until he's right on top of me. He grabs me by the throat. He backs me up against the wall. "Did you forget everything I taught you? That's not how we do things."

When I stayed with him, he ordered me to call him sir. He ordered me to obey him without question.

And he brutalized me and broke my heart. Not with his physical punishments – those were harsh, but a sick part of me craved them. No. What broke my heart was his emotional cruelty, and how he cast me aside without a second thought when I finally dared to defy him.

And now he's back, after I've been gone for two months. Why now? Why at all?

His hand starts to tighten. Just a little.

"I'm sorry. Sir. Is that what you want to hear?" But there's no deference in my voice like there once was.

"I must admit, I miss the sound of that." His lips twist up in a cruel smile that reaches his eyes this time, and he drops his hand. He places his hands on the wall on either side of me, caging me in.

I breathe in his scent of cologne and masculine musk, and a flood of arousal washes over me and threatens to drown me. My nipples are swollen to sensitive nubs, rubbing against the thin fabric of my T-shirt.

I clear my throat and take a deep breath, trying to draw strength into my body and soul.

"Wh-wh-why are you here?" I never stammer around anyone else. Sergei snatches away all my self-confidence. I look up into his ice-blue eyes. "Our agreement has expired."

"No, our agreement hasn't expired. You left three days early."

I don't bother to argue with him, or beg, or plead. Sergei's feelings for me, his behavior towards me, have never made any sense. I don't think even he understands it – and that's why he gets so angry with me.

Behind him I see the wall clock. 5:55 a.m. Six minutes until I'm supposed to call Anastasia. They're sitting in a hotel somewhere, waiting. When I don't call, they'll go on the run. What I need to do right now is stall him. Give Anastasia and the kids time to put as much distance between him and them as possible.

"You want me to finish out the last three days?" I ask him cautiously.

He scoffs. "Is that what you think? You think you can just violate an agreement with me and then change your mind?"

Panic flares in me. When I was forced to live in his mansion in April, he killed a woman just for lying to him. What will he do to me? I used to think I knew him a little, but when he refused to let me go back to him, I realized that he was a stranger to me. I have no way of guessing what his next move will be.

How do you reason with a murdering psychopath who gets off on pain?

When I was serving out my thirty days in his mansion, I tried just about everything. I tried to be obedient and respectful. I tried to be kind and understanding. I tried to fight back. I tried to reason with him.

The only thing I didn't try was outright seduction.

Would it work?

Only one way to find out.

I bite my lip.

"I...I missed you," I whisper, and I'm shaking. I can't even look him in the eyes when I say it. I've brushed up on a lot of my skills over the last couple of months, but I have never been a good liar.

He's a stone statue, untouchable, unmoving. "You missed me so much you went into hiding? If you'd missed me, you knew where to find me."

I don't bother to remind him that when I tried to call him, he all but said he'd kill me if I went back.

He's here. He hasn't killed me...yet. There is still hope.

He moves his hand from my throat and cups my chin. He forces my face up so I have to look him right in the eye. "What did you miss about me, little Willow?" The cynical gleam in his eyes says that he knows that I'm lying.

I've seen what he does to people who lie to him.

"I...I missed when you punished me." I whisper. And that's the truth. Unfortunately.

"Did you really, now?" His hand tightens on my chin, and he jerks my head up even higher. I gasp in fear.

"Yes." I choke on the word.

He drops his hand and takes a step back. "Well, I think we can arrange to make up for lost time." He starts unbuckling his belt, and instantly my mind races back to those times in his playroom, when I quivered with fear and anticipation.

Everything else drops away from me. My worry for my family, for myself... I'm a terrible person. Every cell in my body is singing with anticipation. I want this, I want this...

"Turn around. Pull your pants down and step out of them."

I obey, my hands shaking with eagerness rather than fear.

He slides his fingers into my panties and strokes me lightly. I jump.

"You kept yourself bare for me. Good."

He strapped me down and had me waxed the first day I went to him. He likes me clean-shaven. For some reason, I've stayed in the habit, shaving myself regularly. And whenever I do, I picture him kneeling between my legs the way he did that day, lapping at me with his tongue.

And of course I'm wet. My body always betrays me. It chooses Sergei over self-respect. It wants him to punish my flesh with stinging blows and then thrust into me until I scream for release.

He slides my panties down, and when they fall to my ankles, I step out of them, in a trance.

"T-shirt," he growls.

I take it off and drop it on the floor.

"Bra."

I unhook it and drop it. I'm standing before him naked, and he's fully clothed, just like always. I feel a twinge of sorrow. It's a barrier to intimacy. It makes me feel like a whore.

"Lift your hands over your head."

I do, stretching them, shivering in the air-conditioned chill. I feel goose pimples pebbling my skin.

"I'm c-c-cold," I stammer.

He ignores that. "Turn around." He looks me up and down, and I can feel the heat of his gaze on my naked skin.

I pirouette in a slow circle, and as I do, I glance at the clock again. Five minutes have gone by.

Anastasia will be waiting for my call right now. Within minutes, if she follows the plan, they'll grab their bags and flee.

I also see that he's pulled his belt out, holding it in his hands, and he's hard. The thick length of his cock is outlined perfectly against the fabric of his pants.

He sheds his jacket, tosses it onto a chair. The blue-gray silk of his shirt caresses the swell of his biceps.

"Did you miss me at all?" I ask, my voice little more than a whisper. I brace myself for cruel laughter. He gives me nothing; just a hard, indifferent stare.

"What do you think?" He arches an eyebrow.

My gaze drops to the floor. "I don't know. I never have any idea what's in your head."

"That's right. And that's the way I like it. Now bend over. Hands on the bed."

I do, and I clutch the bedspread so hard that my knuckles are white.

He walks over and trails his hands over my bare ass, between my cheeks, lightly grazing over my pussy.

Then he kicks my legs wider apart. I stagger but keep my hold on the bedspread.

He just stands there for what feels like an eternity. Then his voice behind me makes me jump. "I'd tell you that it's only going to hurt for a minute, but that would be a lie."

FOUR

Bastard.

"Ten lashes. Count for me, Willow." His voice is less harsh than I remembered, more like a caress than a snarling command, but no less terrifying.

He snaps the belt across my ass, a diagonal slash of pain running from the bottom of my left butt cheek to the top of my right cheek. I jump involuntarily and shriek.

"One!" I cry out.

I feel the familiar rush of heat pooling low in my belly, and the moisture of my desire oozing between my pussy lips.

He waits a few seconds before he strikes me again, and I'm forced to remember how a single second can stretch into eternity. Sergei is never predictable. He controls the pace. Like a deadly, weaving cobra, you never know when he'll strike.

The second blow criss-crosses the first, and I jerk and whimper. "Two!"

"Did you really think that you could escape from me, Willow?"

Smack! My flesh quivers under the blow. Three red lines of pain burning across my skin.

"Three!" I gasp for breath. "I didn't think you'd bother to come after me!"

Three slashes in quick succession, so fast that I'm left breathless. My ass is on fire.

"Four, five, six!" I wail.

He pauses to stroke me between my legs. His fingers are soft and gentle, trailing along my heated flesh, which already aches for him. "You love it, don't you?"

The familiar frustration wells up inside me. It's not enough for him to punish me physically. He has to get inside my head and stir with a blender. "Yes, sir. I love it when you touch me. And I hate your guts. Am I still calling you sir?"

"You know, I'll leave that up to you. Some things have changed between us. You changed them. You're more powerful than you know, Willow." His voice is gentle, which means he's going to hurt me.

Two more slashes. I gasp out the numbers. "Seven, eight!" I writhe, squirming. I feel as if flames are licking my skin.

Snap!

"Nine!" Almost over. Please, let it end. "You have all the power here!" I gasp. "You punish me as much as you want, as long as you want, whenever you want, and I can't stop you!"

"Yes, that's true. And you still love it. You crave it. The pain makes the pleasure so much more intense, doesn't it?"

It's so true. Pain and pleasure are twined around each other in my head now, like threads twisting to make a rope. I need both.

Snap!

My flesh quivers beneath the belt, and my whole body jerks.

"Ten!" I cry out, and stand up, frantically rubbing my burning skin.

"Did I say you could stand up?" His harsh breath is right in my ear.

I sneak another glance at the clock. A few more minutes have passed. It's after six a.m. now. They're on the road.

"No. Did I ask permission?" I spin around to face him. "As far as I'm concerned, we're done. You had no right to make me pay for my uncle's debt in the first place, and when you—"

He shoves me up against the wall, pressing against me, a giant wall of body heat and muscle. I feel his rigid cock pressing into my belly.

He cradles my face in his hands and kisses me. His tongue forces its way into my mouth and takes control, swirling, and I nearly swoon. I melt into him. The entire time he held me prisoner, he never kissed me once. All those times he fucked me…his mouth never touched mine.

Now it seems he's making up for lost time. The kiss goes on and on, and he tastes sweet and warm. I never want it to end. I'd starve and die before I tore away from him. Pure pleasure flows from him and into me, through our connected flesh. He's hungry, devouring me. My tongue swirls around his in an intimate dance.

Finally he pulls away from me, and there is a dark, feral look of hunger on his face. Without him holding me up, I stumble. My knees are weak, and I can feel the pain of the belt marks pulsing in time to my heartbeat.

"On the bed, now," he barks at me. "On your back. Legs spread open, knees bent. Make me tell you twice, and your punishment will be fifty lashes." He advances towards me until I'm backed up against the bed. "I'll beat you until you pass out. Then I'll revive you and finish the job."

I'm drowning in an ocean of lust. Why? His threats are sick, they're terrible. I will never understand why fear and pain are such an aphrodisiac for me.

In moments like these, he could make me do anything. My will is not my own; his words are my will.

I fall backwards onto the bed and spread my legs, drawing up my knees.

He starts kissing and licking his way down my stomach, and I hear him unzipping his pants as he's doing it. Somehow, he's shucked them by the time he's between my legs, and kicked off his shoes and socks. He has a condom in his hand and he's rolling it onto the thick column of his phallus that points straight up at the ceiling. Still wearing his shirt, though. Have I ever seen him without a shirt? It's like if he got completely naked in front of me, he'd be baring his soul as well as his body.

"Sweet, sweet Willow." His words caress me, his tongue laps at me, as the burning stripes of his punishment glow on my ass.

I stifle a moan. He moves to suck on my clitoris while one finger curves inside me, stroking my inner wall. It always finds exactly the right spot.

"Oh, God," I wail. "Yes. Oh, please. Please." What am I begging for? I don't even know. I'm mindless, desperate. I've been starving for him for so long now. And he must feel the same way, from the way he's devouring me, with small nips and the swirling lap of his tongue.

He moves up, and I stifle a groan of frustration, because I want his mouth on me forever. He keeps sliding up until he's lying on top of me. He grabs my hands and pins them above my head.

I want to grab the perfect globes of his hard, muscular ass and pull him into me. I want to control the pace, to drive him into me until he pierces my core.

"Let me touch you," I beg.

"Who's in charge?" he says sternly.

"You." It comes out as a sob.

"Don't ever forget it."

And then, to punish me for being needy, he slides into me ever so slowly. Inch by inch. Pushing into my tight tunnel, keeping my wrists pinned as I arch my back and thrust up towards him.

"Please. I want it." I'm a shameless, pathetic beggar.

He stops, halfway inside me. "I know. You always have. From the moment you first saw me."

It's true, and it infuriates me that he's so smug about it. He uses my feelings against me, taunts me for craving him. "I hate you!" I scream at him.

"Music to my ears."

And with that, he thrusts into me so hard that I slide back on the bed.

Pause. He settles down, the hard wall of his chest crushing my breasts, his mouth on my ear.

The he starts pumping, slowly, his breath harsh, drawing out the sweet, evil torture.

He brings me to the brink, and then *stops*. Buried to the hilt. I'm on fire, burning to death from the inside out.

"Who's in charge?" he asks again.

"You are," I sob. "Please, please, please…"

He must like that, because he starts thrusting again, pumping into me, hard and fast, until I shudder convulsively and feel myself shatter. Wave after wave crashes over me, hard, and I'm crying and thrashing underneath him, and he goes rigid. He groans in release, his fingers tightening, then finally relaxes.

He slides out of me, lying there, breathing hard. He is next to me but not touching me. Not looking at me. A million miles away.

I feel a familiar wave of sorrow and loneliness wash over me, just like it did back at his beautiful mansion by the sea.

I let my eyes drift closed and pretend I'm falling asleep. I force myself not to sneak looks at the clock, instead counting out the minutes in my head. I count one Mississippi, two Mississippi... I count to sixty ten times.

And then I feel him sit up. Naptime is over.

I keep my eyes closed, dragging this out as long as possible.

When I feel him shift impatiently, I open my eyes and glance up at him. "You always make me feel horrible after we have sex."

He actually looks puzzled. "How? I didn't say a word, just now."

"Exactly." I lie there, letting the dull, heavy weight of my aching need settle in on me. "You make me feel like a used condom. Something dirty and tainted, for you to come in and cast aside."

He sighs, stroking my face, brushing hair out of my eyes. That tender touch...it heals me and shatters me at the same time. It's rarer and more precious than platinum. "You are not dirty or tainted."

Please be like this forever.

"Once, you held me in your arms. For hours." That was after his friend Feodyr dragged me to that nightmare rape-torture orgy that I barely escaped.

"Yes." He gazes down into my eyes, and his finger slides along my cheek.

I bite my lip. "I still dream about that. I remember how it felt." Tears fill my eyes and I look at the wall, blinking hard. "I felt safer and more...loved, more cared for, then I've felt in years. Maybe ever."

What I'm saying is true, but it's also calculated. I've been obsessively studying survival skills, and this is just one of them. Make your captor care for you, and he's less likely to kill you.

I tried it before with Sergei, and it didn't seem to work at the time, but now I realize that it did work, just very slowly.

Oh, he's still dangerous and unpredictable, and he could still be the death of me. But I've learned to read his moods, and this is the most open, the most reachable, I've ever seen him.

He twines a lock of my hair around his finger. Like a normal man. Like a lover, not a jailer. "You know it has nothing to do with you. It's me. What does love look like? I've never seen it, so I don't know. My parents were drunken beasts who beat and clawed at each other. I grew up on the streets of the most dangerous neighborhood in St. Petersburg. I grew up among thieves and whores. Sex has never been about love for me. It's a biological need, like eating, and once I satisfy it, I don't need it anymore until the next time." He sighs. "Or at least, that's the way it was until I met you."

I hate that anyone had to grow up like that, but it doesn't excuse his horrible treatment of me.

I stare at him, and my gaze is unforgiving. "You're a grown man, Sergei. Your past is your past. You can't blame it for how you behave today."

And I see the steel shutters descend behind his eyes.

Something happened to him long ago, something that made him hate my family. Bringing up the past was a dangerous mistake.

"My past shapes my present."

He slides out of bed abruptly, and stands up. Still wearing his shirt, but naked from the waist down. His thick cock dangles from a dark nest of curly hair, and my gaze is drawn to the hard muscles of his massive thighs before I look up at his face again.

He's retreated from me, and I can't touch him anymore. Sweet Sergei is gone; cold Sergei is back.

"Get dressed. You're coming back with me." He starts pulling on his boxer shorts and pants.

I wonder where Anastasia and Yuri and Helenka are now.

"Can I take a shower?" I ask. Stalling a little more.

He shrugs. "Make it quick."

I hurry into the tiny bathroom and shower for as long as I dare. The water is luke-warm, and the hotel shampoo smells like cheap fruity perfume. When I come out, I get dressed and we leave the room.

His men have been waiting outside for him the whole time. I recognize Jasha, Maks and Slavik. His most loyal foot-soldiers. They'd do anything for him, no questions asked.

Slavik has a bandage across his nose and two black eyes, I notice. That's the kind of life these men lead.

There's a dark car with tinted windows waiting in the parking lot. The last time I stepped into a car like that, I was subjected to a month of terror and ecstasy that broke me apart. Every choice was stripped from me. I became a flesh puppet, jerked about for the amusement of my cruel master. *Never again*, I vow to myself.

I slide my glance over to Sergei as he slams the motel room shut behind him, and I try to mentally calculate how far Anastasia and the kids could have gotten by now. Sergei still hasn't asked me about them. He doesn't care about them, never has. He thinks I'll just walk away from them without a word. He thinks I'll just let him take me back to his house, that giant, beautiful torture palace, so we can resume our cruel dance.

Let him think that for a while longer.

FIVE

I picked the motel for its strategic location. It's always busy around here, which makes it harder for anyone to drag me into a car kicking and screaming without anyone noticing.

We're right across the street from a twenty-four-hour diner. "I'm starving," I say. "I didn't get a chance to eat today." That's a lie, so I stare at the diner as I say it, rather than at Sergei. "Could we go over there and grab some lunch before we hit the road? I feel like I'm about to be sick." I'm trying to make it compelling. If he thinks I'm merely uncomfortable, he may not care.

He shrugs. "I'll send Maks to get you something."

I give him a skeptical glance. "Are you afraid I'll try to call out for help if we go into a restaurant?" But I keep my voice light and non-threatening.

"Maybe." He glances at Maks, who shakes his head in annoyance and heads across the street.

"Grilled cheese and fries! And a chocolate shake!" I yell at Maks. Maks doesn't bother to look back; he just raises his fist to give me a middle-finger salute.

"Keep your voice down," Sergei says, with a pleasant smile that doesn't fool me at all. "Stop trying to draw attention to yourself."

He gestures at a bench by a lamppost, and I sit down. Jasha and Sergei settle down on either side of me, a pair of giant bookends squeezing me between them. Slavik stands next to the bench with his arms folded, constantly scanning the street. Always expecting the worst, seeking out all the potential hiding spots where Sergei's enemies might lie in wait. The rooftops, the alleys, the doorways – in Sergei's world, they're not part of the architecture. They're camouflage for snipers.

I've lived like that myself ever since we went on the run, and it's exhausting. It paints the world around you in an ugly light.

But I'm happy to see there's a line of people out the door of the diner, and Maks is at the end. This should take a while.

I push my hair out of my eyes and blow out an exasperated breath. "Why would I try to escape? I think we've already established that you can find me anywhere. How exactly did you find me again?"

Sergei shrugs and brushes aside the question of how he tracked me down. "If you made a big enough ruckus, if you called for the police, it would draw unwanted attention to me. That's not ideal for a man in my line of work. Mind you, I'm more cautious than your uncle. My businesses are all clean. An audit would turn up nothing. But still…I like my privacy."

If he wants privacy, he'd better not try to drag me into his car.

What he doesn't know is, I'm not going with him. I'm not going back to that beautiful prison, where I'm at the mercy of his cruel moods.

I'm done with being a prisoner. I'm done living my life as a victim of my genetics.

Yes, I was born into a family of drug dealers and illegal arms dealers.

But that was them, not me. I never wanted any part of it. I didn't even find out what we really did for a living until after my parents died and I moved in with my uncle. Vilyat was far less cautious about keeping his activities secret, and I stumbled on the truth when I was home from college.

I was horrified – but I was also trapped. My family was extremely controlling, and for me to leave, I would have had to go into hiding, with no money and no job skills.

I considered running when I found out, but I also saw how my aunt was slipping into a medicated haze, and how much my cousins needed me.

Well, no more. They're free, and I'm done. I would rather die than live life as a slave.

After all, what would happen to me if I went back to Sergei's house? He's got some hidden agenda, and I have no idea what he plans to do to me.

I know that if I run, he is very likely to hunt me down and kill me. In his world, letting someone wiggle their way out of an agreement calls for retribution. If he doesn't come after me, he's admitting weakness. So he wouldn't even have a choice, not if he wants to stay at the top of the heap. It's him or me.

I'm not suicidal. Far from it. I'm terrified.

But if I disappear behind those white stucco walls again, I'm afraid I'll never emerge.

I don't trust this version of Sergei, because his moods are mercurial, shifting without warning or reason. Yes, so far he's been less cruel – at least out here in the open. But first and foremost he's a warrior, and everything he does is strategic. He's trying to lull me into a sense of false security, and the second I slide into his darkened vehicle, he'll go right back to the way he was, or worse.

"Why do you even want me back?" I ask him in a low voice. "You were holding me for collateral. My uncle already cut and ran; you know he's not going to pay you and he doesn't care if you torture me and then serve me up as stew." Maybe I shouldn't give Sergei any ideas. I clear my throat and forge ahead. "I have no value to you anymore."

He ignores me, staring straight ahead.

"How is Lukas?" I ask.

He gives me a nasty look. "Fine. I make sure of that, every day. But you left him behind, so you've lost the right to ask about his welfare."

Now I'm pissed.

"You told me I'd never be allowed to see him again, even though you knew it would hurt him deeply, so don't try to make me feel bad about leaving. If I'd stayed, I still wouldn't have been allowed to see him, you hypocritical motherfucker. Any pain that child is suffering, you are one hundred percent responsible for," I snap at him.

He nods. "Fair point."

Well, this is something. He's actually letting me disagree with him, without threatening me or brutalizing me.

But it's not enough, and it's much too late.

And we fall silent.

The silence stretches on and on. The sun is rising higher in the sky and heat shimmers up from the sidewalk. Sweat rolls down my forehead and stings my eyes, and I wipe it with the back of my hand. I can't remember where my fake glasses are. I'm not wearing makeup anymore. I didn't style my hair in waves this morning, and the dark color is starting to fade. Willow is re-emerging, and Sarah is fading.

I wonder what kind of disguise I'll use when I escape this time.

If I escape.

I pass the time dreaming up new hair colors. New looks. Red. Platinum blonde. Green contact lenses? Brown contact lenses?

None of his men speak a word. People glance at them as they walk by. They can't help it; Sergei and his men demand attention without trying. They're too big, too dangerous, to blend in. They're like a pride of lions moving through a herd of gazelles.

Maks finally brings the food back to me. When I thank him, he mutters, "Fuck yourself" in Russian.

"Better than fucking you," I reply, also in Russian. "At least I know I'll come." That last bit is in English. Jasha chokes on a laugh, and I see Sergei's lips twitch in an almost-smile.

I force myself to eat, taking my time between each bite. I chew slowly and thoroughly. I'm too nervous to eat much.

Then I walk over to a garbage can, and Sergei comes with me, attached to me like an enormous shadow. I toss the fast food containers in. His men are standing about twenty feet away, watching us, scanning the crowd, always aware of their surroundings. I glance back at the parking lot. The dark car has moved to the sidewalk now, and its motor is running.

"You weren't that hungry after all," Sergei says, looking mildly amused. Damn it, he knows I'm stalling – I'm sure of it now. I feel a shiver of unease.

But a crowd of people are walking towards us, and I have my chance. Probably my only chance.

"I'm leaving," I inform him.

"You really think so?" He cocks his head to the side, looking at me with polite interest.

"I know so. And you want to know why?"

"Not particularly."

I snort. "Remarks like that are a big part of the reason I'm not coming back. Because you treat me like crap, and I'm so over it. I don't care that you and I have the most amazing sex ever."

"Well, thank you, Willow, that's so sweet of you." His lip curls up in a smirk.

I plow on. "Don't interrupt me. I was willing to live up to the agreement that my uncle made for me, even though you punished me and abused me for things I never did. I sat there while you insulted me, knocked me around, humiliated me like I was a streetwalker – and I would have taken it all. But I never agreed to let the abuse extend to my family. When you locked me away from my cousins, that ended us."

"I see."

He should be threatening me more. He's being too calm. It worries me.

I plow on. He's just trying to psych me out. He can't take me here in front of all these people. Unlike Feodyr, he's not the type to murder innocent bystanders, and he also has plans for his future. He's not a suicidal nutjob. He has no choice but to let me go.

"You haven't even said what you expect of me now, but I don't care. I have no reason to stay with you, with the way you treat me. And I will never forgive you for keeping me from my family."

He nods. "Understandable."

What the hell? Why isn't he threatening me? I know he didn't come all this way just to let me smart off to him and then walk away.

The crowd is moving past me now, and this is my chance. I leap to my feet and muscle my way into the middle of the crowd as they hurry across the street to make the light.

I glance behind me, heart hammering against my ribcage. Sergei and his men are walking behind the group.

When we get to the other side, I make a break and run for it. Fear makes me lighter than air. I dash down the street, down the block, around a corner. Now I'm right across the street from a police kiosk. I know where all of them are.

Sergei and Maks come pounding up behind me. The dark car glides up to the curb in front of me and idles there. Jasha and Slavik come shooting out of an alleyway and block my path.

People are looking at us warily.

I glare at Sergei. "You don't want attention? Then get the hell away from me, now. Off this street. Out of my life. Otherwise..." I glance across the street at the police kiosk. "You have no idea how loud I can scream."

"Oh, I think I do." He smirks when he says that, and Jasha chortles. Motherfucking fuck-faces. When Sergei took me to his playroom and punished me, he played it over the intercom so his men could hear my cries.

Well, that's not going to happen again. *I am never coming back with you*," I rage at him. Why the hell isn't he taking me more seriously? "You'll have to kill me first."

"Perhaps this will change your mind," Sergei says to me.

Maks waves a computer tablet at me, and my heart stutters in my chest. I should have known that Sergei wouldn't let me slip through his fingers that easily. He didn't get to where he is today by letting amateurs like me get the jump on him.

Maks thrusts the tablet right in front of my face. My aunt Anastasia's frightened face looks back at me.

"Willow, they have us. I'm so sorry," she whispers.

Sergei has had them all along. While he was whipping me, while we were having sex, while I was pretending to sleep, while I was showering, while I was eating.

He let me think I was in control, then snatched the control away from me. He was toying with me, a tomcat gently batting a mouse between its enormous paws before he sinks his fangs in.

The sidewalk seems to move beneath my feet, and I stagger, and Sergei puts his hand on my shoulder to steady me.

A cloud slides over the sun, and I feel darkness closing in on me. He's stolen everything from me. My family. My freedom. My future.

I will never escape this life.

SIX

SERGEI

Her eyes are enormous blue pools of grief and fury. She sways where she stands, and my hand on her shoulder holds her up. I like that she can't stand without my help. She needs me.

I win. I own her again.

But guilt poisons my relief. Willow is the only person in the world who can make me feel guilty. Before I met her, I couldn't even have described what that emotion felt like.

"*No,*" she whispers desperately, to a cruel, uncaring universe.

I gesture at the car.

"Fun time's over. Get the fuck in the car."

She meets my gaze with a genuine disgust that burns into my soul. When she looks at me like that, it makes me loathe myself. Me, the man without a conscience. Bile rises in my throat, and I swallow it down.

Her voice trembles. "If we go back there, you'll just lock them up and hurt them all over again. No. I'm going to the police and telling them that you kidnapped them. I'm done with your sick games."

I swat aside her threats. "You against the billionaire? You against all the resources I have? The police would never be able to prove a thing, and they would never find a trace of them."

She sucks in a gulping breath. She's shaking all over.

Will she surrender to me? Have I stripped her of her last bit of free will?

Tears are streaming down her face, and her breath comes out in wordless sobs, each one jerking her slim body.

I realize that I don't want to know who will win this fight. The cost of victory would be too high.

So I give a little.

I never, ever do that for anyone.

Only for my Willow.

She won't be mine for long, but I want to enjoy what time I have with her, and if I push her too hard, if I break her, I'll spend all our time together sick with self-disgust.

So I let her know the deal has changed. I tick off my conditions. "You will come back with me for thirty days. When you left, you restarted the clock. I will allow you to spend all the time you want with your family. You can see Lukas again too. In exchange, you will spend your nights with me, and you will treat me with respect in front of my men. At the end of the thirty days, I'm leaving the country forever. You will be free of me. You can keep the house. You can live there with your family if you want."

She stares at me in shock. "Keep your house? What? Are you crazy?"

"Hello, have you met me? Of course I'm crazy. And yes. I will give you the house. And cash to live off. Beats working at a diner for the rest of your life, doesn't it?"

"But I…" she shakes her head as if trying to dislodge my words.

"I already told you I wouldn't accept dirty money."

"If I could prove to you that the money that purchased that house was clean, would you accept it then?" The house cost me twenty million dollars. She'd be a fool to turn it down.

"I would never believe you. And why do you want me in the first place? You could get all the beautiful women in the world. Women who are way prettier and actually want to be there with you."

"You don't give yourself enough credit, Willow."

She glares at me. "Is that actually your attempt at a compliment? That's really the best you can do?"

She's right. She deserves so much more. Unfortunately, what she deserves – decency, kindness, lavish praise – I can't give her.

Instead, I give her the best gift I am capable of giving – a little bit of honesty.

"I'm working on some things," I say in a low voice. "A final project. And I can't think straight without you. I can't concentrate without you there. You've gotten under my skin like nobody I've ever met before. I didn't want it to happen, but it did. I'm distracted. I'm making mistakes. So for the sake of my end game, I need you with me until...until I'm finished."

Tears spill down her cheeks. She glares at me. "And then what happens at the end of the thirty days? You're magically cured of the disgusting disease that is me?"

I brush the tears from her cheek with my thumb, and she gives that shudder of helpless desire that makes me want to take her right there, on the nearest bench.

"Willow. You're an addiction without a cure. But once I've accomplished what I need to, it doesn't matter what happens to me. So if losing you means I end up totally fucked in the head, it'll be fine. *After* I do what I need to."

She shakes her head slowly. "If I affect you that way...why wouldn't you try to keep me forever?" Then she sniffs hard and wipes away the tears with the back of her hand. "Not that I'm saying I want to stay. I'm just trying to understand this."

"I won't try to keep you, because I don't deserve you. I could never make you happy. I've never had a normal relationship in my life. I don't have normal friends, I have street soldiers. I don't have normal relationships, I have sex with gold-diggers or whores, and then I give them money to go away."

And I haven't given a lot of thought to what will happen once I've destroyed the last men who were responsible for my younger brother's death. I haven't planned for a life beyond that. I'm afraid to think of life beyond that.

I will still have a business to run, but will I be able to motivate myself to get up in the morning, once the last man on my list is dead? Maybe I'll let myself spin out of control, and give the business to my men. God knows they've earned it.

"You could have tried to make me happy. Back before you said and did such terrible things to me." Her voice is small. She's ashamed of hinting, even in a subtle, roundabout way, that she wants to stay with me.

I nod. "I know. But you know what I am, Willow."

Now anger pushes aside her sorrow. That's better. I like Willow angry. I like the fight, the resistance. "Yes, I do know what you are. You paraded me around in front of your men half naked. You let them look at me like that. You insulted me again and again, while everyone watched."

I taste metal in my mouth and swallow, but the bad taste won't go away. "Yes. It was a means to an end. To hurt your uncle and weaken him further. I won't apologize for it, but it will not happen again when you come home with me."

Come home with me. The words taste bittersweet. *Come home with me, stay with me…*

The car is idling right next to us, and there's nobody standing near us. The old rage is rising up inside me. When I let her reach those soft, yearning places that never existed inside me before I met her…it makes me panic. It makes me lash out at her.

I've given her too much already. She can't steal any more of my soul.

My voice goes harsh. From zero to asshole in no time flat, that's me.

"And now we're done. You have five seconds to say yes or no. If you don't give me the answer I want, I will throw you in that car, and take you back to my house, and things will go back to the way they were before. And I'll have no compunction at all about using your family to hurt you. You already know that."

She glares at me. I'm not giving her any choice, and she's furious, and helpless.

And fuck me if it doesn't make my dick hard.

I really need professional help.

"Five, four, three…" I count fast.

"Yes!" she snaps at me.

I open the door of the car, and she throws herself in, looking out of the opposite window, avoiding my gaze.

I slide in next to her and slam the door shut, swallowing her up in my trap.

She sits stiffly, pressed up against the door, as far away from me as she can get. It doesn't matter. For now, I'll let her have that illusion of freedom, because I know the truth. If I wanted to, I could have her right here in the car, and she'd come so hard she cried.

The car takes us to a small airport, where a private plane is waiting for us.

"Where is my family?" she demands as we walk towards it.

"They already left, on a separate plane. We'll meet them back there."

"They'd *better* be back there, and they'd better be unharmed." Her threats have no more strength then a puff of air, but she's brave and foolish and desperate.

The look she gives me could scorch a lesser man. But as we climb aboard the plane, I am calm and at peace for the first time since she left me.

I have my Willow back.

* * *

It's evening, and we're back at my house on the coast. Like every decision of mine, the purchase of this home was a strategic one.

I was moving in on Vilyat, so I wanted to be relatively close to him, but not too close. The house was a couple of hours from his. And I needed a house that would also serve as a fortress. This house had no close neighbors and was easily defensible. Security cameras everywhere, and impossible to sneak up on.

I take them on the tour when we arrive. I want to show Willow, without words, that things will be different this time around.

As we walk through the house, she and Anastasia and the kids huddle together, a tight, angry unit, shutting me out. Anastasia has her hands on her kids' shoulders, as if that could keep them safe if I should choose to snatch them away from her.

The contrast between Willow and Anastasia is a sharp one. Anastasia is a sultry goddess who glides through life with sensual grace. She's not even trying; she's just got those curves and that Marilyn Monroe roll to her hips. Willow is small and slender and quiet, with wary eyes. She's the girl who stands at the back of the room, doing her best to blend in to the wallpaper. She's pretty in that friend's-younger-sister way.

Inside, though…inside she's the most beautiful thing I've ever come across. She's sweet and strong. She still lets herself love – fearlessly, passionately. She puts everyone else's needs before her own; I wish she wouldn't do that. I wish she'd love herself as much as she loves her family, and every little wounded bird she finds.

She's braver than anyone I know. No matter how terrified she is, she'll fight like a tigress for everyone but herself. Like Lukas – she fought for him, knowing it would cost her terribly. I know that when she was working at diner and watching every penny, she'd buy meals and hand them out to the homeless on her way back to her apartment.

And I know she cares about me. Loves me, even, or at least thinks she does. I can't put a name to the way that I feel about her, because it would make it too real.

The first place I take them is the workshop I've set up for Yuri, where he can build robots and model cars. I know he loves to tinker.

His eyes light up when he sees the shelves of robot kits and model toy kits, the work table, the tools.

"This is really just for me? It's all mine?" he cries.

His sister glares and shoves him. "Have you forgotten what he did to us?" Helenka snaps at him. "His men just put their guns in our faces and made us get in his car. You remember how he treated us when we were here before? Every time we asked to see Willow or Mom, he lied and said they were busy. He's a *liar*. He's a bully. He's a kidnapper. We're his prisoners."

Yuri's face falls. He's like a balloon that's been pricked, his happiness leaking out.

"Dad never let me do this kind of stuff," he says glumly, casting a longing glance at all the wonderful toys I've bought for him. "He said it was for peasants."

Anastasia bites her lip and stares at the floor. She's still furious with me; understandable. My men did kidnap her and her kids at gunpoint. But I don't give a fuck. I would do it all over again, and worse things, to get Willow back.

Willow winces at Yuri's dismay and pats Helenka on the arm. "Hey. I'm not saying that we forgive Sergei, but that's a separate issue. Please let Yuri enjoy this. Don't make him feel bad. It's incredibly cool, and Yuri has real talent. He could be an engineer someday. He could design cars, or…or space robots."

Now Yuri beams. I know how he feels. Willow is like the sun, and when she beams her light at you, it can warm the coldest heart.

Next, I take them into a gymnasium. Helenka loves gymnastics and self-defense classes. There's all kinds of climbing equipment and mats. There are also punching bags and hand wraps for boxing, and various pads and helmets for self-defense training.

Jasha is in there, leaning against the wall. Nobody is better at hand-to-hand combat than him. Not even me, and I'm pretty fucking lethal.

"Jasha will train you while you're here," I tell Helenka.

"Can I play in here?" Yuri begs.

"Nope. It's mine." Helenka's still sullen and resentful. Then again, what thirteen-year-old American girl isn't? She has no idea what a glorious life she leads.

"If I can play in here, you can make laser death-ray robots with me," he says with a winning smile.

Helenka gives me a cold sideways glance. "Okay. I guess we could use them to burn Sergei like a bug."

I roll my eyes. "You can continue your Krav Maga lessons, since those are your favorite," I tell her.

She meets my gaze fearlessly. She's like a miniature Willow.

"You're making a mistake teaching me how to fight back. When I get good enough, I'm going to kick your ass for what you've done to us."

Willow chokes back a laugh behind her hand.

I look at Anastasia. She has a quiet smile of pride on her face. She's a different woman from the stumbling, mumbling drug addict I saw just a couple of months ago.

"You can join your children in self-defense classes," I say to her. "I've got a laptop set up for you as well, so you can continue taking your computer classes without interruption."

"You'll really let us go at the end of thirty days?" Fear and hope mingle in her soft voice.

I don't do hand-holding. "I'm not going to repeat myself, Anastasia."

Hurt and anger flash across her face, and Willow shoots me an angry look.

Anastasia glances at her niece. "And you won't hurt Willow?"

I'm not going to promise that – because I am going to hurt her, often, but Willow will like it. No, she'll love it. Of course, Anastasia doesn't need to know our little secrets.

"Willow will be fine."

Jasha walks up.

"We will begin our lesson now. We'll work out until dinner." He looks at Helenka. "One rule. You will speak to Sergei with respect."

Anastasia moves in front of her children.

"One other rule," she says. "If you hurt my kids, even accidentally, I swear to God I will tear your throat out with my teeth." The feral gleam in her eyes says she means it. She would die for them. Vilyat nearly extinguished her inner fire, but it's back now, a roaring bonfire, and I don't think she'll ever lose it again.

Jasha gives her a bored look. "Lesson number one," he says to her. "Don't be an idiot. Never tell your enemy what you plan on doing to them."

Helenka has been standing behind him. She suddenly lashes out with a whirling kick that is so fast I barely see it coming, catching Jasha in the back of the knee. He staggers and almost falls.

"Lesson number two, watch how you talk to my mother," she snaps. "Lesson number three, don't underestimate me."

A thirteen-year-old girl who can't weigh more than ninety pounds did that to him.

Willow starts laughing. Yuri joins her. Anastasia is laughing, and so am I. I laugh and laugh, until tears come to my eyes and I'm gasping for breath. I realize I haven't laughed like that, a genuine howl of laughter, in…possibly ever.

Jasha glares at them. His face is flushed with humiliation.

"Let's start with some laps around the mats," he snaps. "All of you. Then pushups until you puke."

"I don't have a jogging bra!" Anastasia protests.

He rakes her with a look of contempt. "Sucks for you, princess," he growls. "When a mugger is chasing you, are you going to stop and ask him to wait while you put on a jogging bra? No? Then start running."

"I need to go make some calls," I say. It's the last thing in the world I want to do. Every cell in my body craves Willow. I want to smell her, taste her, bury myself deep in her tight, warm sheath. That's why I'm forcing myself to leave the room. To prove to myself that I still can.

That's okay. She has no idea what's coming.

She ran away from me. She disobeyed me.

Disobedience requires retribution.

SEVEN

WILLOW

After Jasha's brutal workout, which does indeed bring us all near to barfing, Anastasia and I sit on the sidelines and watch while he works with the children.

Jasha has never been particularly friendly to me, and I keep an eagle eye on him, but I can't fault his treatment of Helenka and Yuri. He doesn't hurt them or even belittle them. He's brusque but efficient. His teaching is excellent, and very tactical. He encourages them to turn their weaknesses into strengths. For instance, they're children, small and slender. That's a weakness. But anyone who doesn't know them will underestimate them. That's a strength.

He has them practice acting helpless and terrified, going limp quickly when he grabs them, and shows them various pressure points where they can strike once they've lulled an attacker into a sense of false security. Several times, I hear him grunt in genuine pain.

"Well, I must say I'm enjoying the show," I say to Anastasia. "If we get lucky, they'll cripple him for life. Helenka's a lot meaner than she looks."

"Yes, she is," Anastasia says with quiet pride. She nods approvingly as Yuri twists out of Jasha's grip. Then she sighs. "This is all bullshit, of course."

I look at her in surprise. "Look at you with your filthy mouth. I didn't know you had it in you, Anastasia."

"I've learned all kinds of fun things while you were at work," she says. She watches them wrestling. "Like strategy. I study strategy. Sergei is trying to fool us into thinking he's helping us, here. But he's also sending a message, that he knows we were taking self-defense classes in Ohio. I mean, he even named the type of class we took. And the same when he mentioned my computer classes. That's a warning. He's telling us there's nowhere that we can run and hide, he'll always be watching us. And also, every single trick that he and his men teach us, they not only know those tricks, but they know how to predict, block, and counter-attack. They would never teach us anything we could really use against them."

Now I'm openly staring at her. I'd figured out all those things, but I've never seen this side of her. "Wow, Anastasia. It's like I don't know you at all."

"You don't." There's a flash of danger in her eyes.

For years, she was this quiet, meek woman who only spoke when spoken to, who screwed her smile on tight and trailed behind her husband with her head down. Now that she's been freed from Vilyat and she's off the prescription opioids, she's turning into something I don't even recognize.

We turn back to watch the kids, and suddenly I'm a little more confident about Helenka and Yuri's future.

I try to think about what I know about her. I remember that when I was nine years old, my parents told me that my uncle Vilyat had gotten married to a girl in Russia, and he was bringing her home to California. They showed me a picture of Vilyat and his new wife, who liked like a Hollywood movie star. She wore tons of makeup and had her hair teased into a big, dramatic updo. She had just graduated from high school. She was eighteen, and Vilyat was thirty-seven.

"*Gross,*" I said when I heard their ages. "I'm never going to marry an old man like that."

"You will marry whoever you're told to!" My father barked at me, and I could feel the anger rolling off him.

"But I get to choose!" I stared at him in shock. That wasn't how life worked.

My father stormed towards me. He'd never hit me, because he'd never had a reason to. I was the perfect daughter; I made sure of it. There was a violence, a rage, that rippled just under the surface of his skin, and even as a very small child, I knew that the only way to be safe in my house was to keep my father happy.

My mother shot to her feet, moving between me and him.

Right then, I knew he wasn't just about to hit me – he was about to kill me. I was light-headed with fear.

"I will talk to her. Demyon. Please. She is just a child. She doesn't know what she's saying."

The undercurrent of terror in my mother's voice stole the breath from my body.

What was happening?

I knew *exactly* what I'd said. I knew what the fairy tales told you. You met a prince and you fell in love with him. You married because you were in love.

She hurried me out of the room. She talked to me, all right, but she did so in whispers. She told me that she'd make sure that my father would never force me to marry anyone, but we had to pretend that I would do whatever he wanted.

That was when she first started planning to buy a secret apartment, to get fake ID for both of us. From what I gathered, as soon as I finished college, my father was going to arrange a marriage for me. If my parents hadn't died in that plane crash, she and I would have vanished right after my graduation ceremony – and before I was sentenced to a lifetime of marital servitude.

I watch Helenka land a hard, savage kick in Jasha's stomach, and a smile curls my lips. Vilyat would never have allowed her to take self-defense lessons. What he would have said was that a woman should be able to depend on her man to protect her. But the truth was, he believed that women should be helpless and scared.

Sergei is a terrible person, and yet he's better to these kids than their father ever was. He took the time to find out exactly what they wanted and needed, and he gave it to them. He let them know that the things they enjoyed weren't silly little hobbies. He encouraged them to pursue their passions, to excel at them. Anastasia, too.

Yeah, he was being a dick and making a point when he let her know that he was aware she had been taking computer classes, but he could just have told us that he knew what we were up to, without giving any of us a damn thing. Instead he built these wonderful rooms for the kids and made sure that my aunt could finish studying and get her online certificate.

No man in our family would have done that; the women and children only existed to be molded into the shape the Toporov men desired.

After our practice session, I go back to my room to shower before dinner, and it's as if I never left. A closet full of beautiful clothes, all brand new, that are exactly the styles I love.

Art supplies on my desk.

And a laptop. That's new.

I wonder how much Sergei knows about what I've really been up to. My aunt and I have both been obsessed with teaching ourselves how to hack, and we've gotten good at it, better than we are at physically defending ourselves. To protect ourselves from our enemies, we needed to know what they were doing. Vilyat has gotten sloppy since Sergei drove him out of the country, and we at least had some idea of his comings and goings.

While we were in Ohio, I also tried to find out anything I could about Sergei. It wasn't easy. He's very careful. He owns many businesses, including an international shipping company based out of a port city in the Leningrad Oblask, a chain of warehouses both here and in Russia, and a construction company.

One day, I managed to hack in to the email of one of his vendors, and they were talking about Vilyat and "Operation Salvat", but they were very vague. The next day when I tried to sign in, I was blocked.

I feel like it has something to do with my family, with whatever plan Sergei has for my two surviving uncles, Vilyat and Edik. For whatever reason, Sergei bears a ferocious hatred for the Toporovs. I want to know why.

I log in to the laptop that Sergei has set up for me and check all the programs on it. There are security programs that I don't recognize. For now, I just do some pointless web-surfing to throw him off track, looking up shoes and turquoise jewelry, and then log off. I could create a virtual private network on there, and I don't think he could see what I was doing on it, but I don't want him to find out my new skill level yet.

That evening, I eat dinner in the dining room with my family. Sergei doesn't join us. I could almost have predicted that. Sergei hates that he needs me, because he sees it as a weakness. He's the type who's into self-denial, and right now he's proving to himself how strong he is by making himself wait until he sees me again.

After dinner, one of the servants takes us to a media room with soft leather chairs, and we pick a science fiction flick to watch on an enormous screen, and eat fresh buttered popcorn delivered by a maid.

The night stretches on and on, and finally we go back to our rooms. I get to see Anastasia, Yuri and Helenka's suite, at the end of a hallway, rooms grouped together.

"You'll sleep in my room," Anastasia declares to her kids, and they don't even argue. A normal thirteen-year-old girl would argue about being treated like a baby. Helenka's life has never been normal.

I head back to my room and toss and turn, wondering if Sergei will come for me. Wondering why he's not there.

In the morning, I wake up with a start. Someone is pounding on my door. The clock says I've slept in until nine a.m. Helenka is yelling something about breakfast.

As I hurry to the door to answer her, I stop short. Someone's been in my room while I was sleeping. Someone has left turquoise necklaces, bracelets, and earrings on the desk next to my computer. On the floor by the desk are at least fifty pairs of shoes; sandals, espadrilles, ballet flats. They're the shoes I was looking at online yesterday afternoon – a pair in every color.

I feel the bars of my gilded cage shrinking in on me.

EIGHT

Day two, morning...

I pull on a pale-pink cotton maxi dress with embroidered flowers at the neckline, and a pair of the macramé sandals that appeared in my room overnight thanks to the Shoe Fairy, and then I join my family.

A silent butler guides us outside. We're served breakfast in the rose garden. We can see the ocean from where we're sitting. There's an obscene amount of food on the table, and we dive into piles of fluffy pancakes and salty bacon and buttery scrambled eggs.

Maks and Jasha sit down with us. Sergei's still not here.

"Do you want some pancakes? They're really good." Yuri asks them politely, and my heart aches. He is such a good kid, despite everything. I mean, he's offering pancakes to his freaking kidnappers.

Maks is curt. "We already ate."

"Then why are you here? Jerkhole?" Helenka snaps at them. Sometimes she gets crabby with her brother, but nobody else is allowed to be rude to him.

Maks fixes his cold gaze on her. "Because it's our job."

I snort in contempt. "I'm just curious," I say to them. "What exactly are you afraid we'll do if you're not watching us? Do you think we're going to dive into the ocean and swim for it? Or try to run for the gates and climb over the razor wire?"

"Would you like to tell me how to do my job, Willow?" Maks grabs a silver coffee urn and pours himself and Jasha some coffee. "I'm all ears. I'm sure you'll have some really good suggestions."

I give him one of the smiles I've learned from Sergei – the smile that doesn't reach the eyes, and says, *I'd rather be stabbing in you in the jugular than talking to you.* "None I could repeat in front of the children."

"Jeez, like I'm five. I've heard people swear before," Helenka says with annoyance.

I wave her off and turn to Anastasia. "So, I was web surfing yesterday, looking at some jewelry and shoes, and this morning when I woke up I found that someone had been in my room and, lo and behold, everything I was searching for online was now by my desk. Someone managed to buy all that stuff, that fast, and sneak it into my room. That's not at all creepy."

She grimaces in sympathy.

Maks bangs his fist down on the table. "Don't insult Sergei's generosity!" he barks at me.

Anastasia looks at him and says something in Russian that makes Jasha choke on his coffee. Maks stares at her in surprise, and actually looks mildly offended. I know conversational Russian, but nobody's taught me the really good insults. Anastasia knows them, apparently.

Seriously. I do not know my aunt *at all*.

Jasha's still coughing.

"I got certified in CPR while I was in Ohio," I say to Jasha. "Ask me if I'd use it to help you if you choked right now. Go on, ask me. Oh wait, you can't, you're choking."

Maks says something in Russian that I partly recognize – something about me being a very cheap prostitute – and he slams down his coffee cup and storms off.

Helenka glares and waves at him as he walks away. "Buh-bye," she says, and then she and Anastasia high-five each other and exchange the kind of secret smile that only mothers and daughters share. It makes me miss my mother so fiercely that tears sting my eyes.

I don't think about my mother very much, because when I do, it feels like the hot jab of a knife in my heart.

My lovely mother, Tatiana. She was soft and strong at the same time, steel wrapped in cotton. I grab my coffee and drain an entire cup, blinking hard, and I wrap the image of my mother up lovingly in her blue comforter and shove her back in the corner of my mind where I keep her memory safe but hidden.

"Willow! Willow!" A familiar voice calls out.

It's Lukas, rushing towards us, followed by his caretakers Kris and Marya. He's wearing Ralph Lauren jeans, expensive leather loafers, and a polo shirt. His cheeks are pink, and he's glowing with health, if not happiness. He's dressed up like a child model in a catalog.

He slows down when he gets to me, and pats my arm. He doesn't try to cling to me like he used to when he first met me. "You are my friend," he tells me, in thickly accented English. "Not mother. Friend."

The look on his face brings tears to my eyes. It's the look of a child whose heart has been broken. When he saw me in the garden in April, he was so sure that I was his mother. I tried at the time to explain to him, gently, that I wasn't, but he refused to believe me.

And then, thanks to Sergei's abuse, I went on the run with my family and vanished for two months, without saying goodbye to him. I hurt Lukas. I made the world feel less safe for him. I didn't mean to, but I can see the pain in his eyes.

I swallow the lump in my throat. "I am your friend, always," I tell him. "How have you been?"

"I am very well, thank you."

He couldn't speak a word of English the last time I saw him. "Your English is excellent, Lukas!"

He lights up, and a little of the sadness fades as he nods vigorously. "Yes. I am learn it very good."

Helenka and Yuri smile at him. How could they not? Lukas is a little bundle of sweetness. He's a walking bag of sugar.

I introduce him to my aunt and cousins. They try to talk to him in Russian, and he looks confused.

"He's Czech," I tell them. "And how is he related to Sergei again?" I ask Jasha. Jasha gives me that stone-faced stare that all of Sergei's men have perfected.

Anastasia looks from Lukas to me and back again, with a tiny frown. Then she shrugs and ruffles his hair with her hand. "He can come play with Helenka and Yuri," she says. She glances at Kris and Marya, who both nod their approval.

"You bring him back after," Kris says to her. Then he says something to Lukas in Czech, probably reminding him to say please and thank you. Kris and Marya leave us.

Lukas' eyes light up with excitement. "I show you the garden? Come, come, I have jungle gym. It is very high!"

We follow him, winding through the sweet perfume of the rose garden, down gravel paths, towards the little house where he and Kris and Marya live. There's an amazing wooden play structure there, shaped like a castle at one end and a space ship at the other. Sergei always buys the best of everything.

Frustration bubbles up inside me. There's a puzzle here. Sergei's part of it, my family is part of it, Lukas is part of it. If only I could figure out where the pieces fit into the whole, I might have a better idea of what Sergei ultimately plans for us.

But I'm not getting any answers this morning.

Anastasia and I watch for a while as all three kids scramble around on the wondrous wooden play structure. I see Helenka at the top, scanning the grounds. Looking for an escape route. I could join her, but I don't bother. We're probably safer here then we would be on our own. If Sergei could find us, then Vilyat could have found us eventually. Also, I've already violated my agreement with Sergei once; I shudder to think what he'd do to me if I did it twice.

Jasha comes to fetch the kids. They'll have another self-defense lesson and then someone will work with Yuri in his new mad science lab. When Lukas hears that he can join them, he bounces with happiness. Anastasia hovers over them protectively, and even holds Lukas' hand as they head off for their lessons.

I go back to my room. The shoes have all been moved to my closet.

I shower, I surf the internet, looking at yachts just to amuse myself and see if Sergei's going to buy everything I look at online. Maybe a yacht will show up tomorrow, moored to one of the palm trees. Finally, I get bored, so I go searching for Sergei. I walk past maids and servants who nod respectfully at me as I pass, and then I hear his voice around a corner, and head towards it.

I'm about to turn the corner when I hear something that freezes me in my tracks.

"That's perfect. You're beautiful, Ludmilla, thank you."

I stand perfectly still.

Who the hell is Ludmilla?

"Fantastic. Great, great. Best news I've heard in ages. I could kiss you."

Could you really? Not if I find the bitch and stab her first.

A wave of jealousy snatches the breath from my lungs. I turn and hurry away before he sees me.

I try to remember if Sergei ever told me I was beautiful.

As I make it back to my room, I realize I'm actually crying. I hurry into the bathroom, and my hands are shaking as I turn on the tap. I grab a washcloth and scrub at my face.

Who the hell is Ludmilla?

This is insane. Sergei has made it abundantly clear that he will leave me for good at the end of thirty days. He's even offered to write me a huge "thank you for letting me fuck you" check in the form of his glorious estate.

He can't possibly care about this woman as much as he cares about me. He admitted it himself; he's obsessed with me. So obsessed he spent a lot of time and money hunting me down and bringing me back to him.

Did he sound passionate on the phone? Could she be a family member? An employee? That must be it.

It has to be.

He brought *me* back here, not her. I know how strong his feelings are for me. I'm not saying they're healthy feelings – they're a dark obsession. But if he has such strong, enormous feelings for me, they must fill up his whole heart. They couldn't possible leave room for anyone else.

That's what I tell myself as I try to wash away the hurt and jealousy that chew at me.

I'm scrubbing and scrubbing at my face when I hear Sergei's voice right behind me.

"Come with me," he says without preamble.

I start and stifle a shriek. I turn off the water and drop the wash cloth, and spin around to stare up at him.

He turns around and walks away. So sure, I'll follow, like the loyal dog I am. And I do. I hurry after him.

"You know, normal people might say something like, hello, how was your day?" I say mildly as I follow him out the door.

"Do I seem like someone who's interested in what normal people say and do?" he asks. His tone isn't harsh, but it's not friendly either.

"What about being interested in how I feel? Like not having someone bark orders at me like I'm a dog all the time?"

He glances back at me. He arches an eyebrow. "Don't lie to me, Willow, because it won't end well. We both know that you love it when I give you orders. It makes your pussy wet for me. It makes your nipples hard."

I flush with embarrassment.

"I like it when you give me orders under certain circumstances," I say quietly. "But when we're not having sex, I enjoy actual conversation."

"I don't need to ask how your day was, because I know what you're doing every second of every minute of the day. And where you are, and who you're doing it with. And I'm not big on idle chit-chat to fill up dead space."

He stops, and I realize that we're at the doorway of his playroom.

He gestures impatiently, and I walk in, emotions roiling inside me. He's given me so much pain and pleasure here. Just walking through the door makes my nipples harden in anticipation.

It's all as I remembered it – the big X-shaped thing with cuffs attached, the whips on a rack on the wall, the shelves of dildos and lubes, the cabinets full of toys, the bed, the structures whose functions I don't even recognize. There's a sink with a rolling cart of towels next to it, and a refrigerator.

We stop in the middle of the room. I want to stall – because whatever he has in mind for me is going to hurt.

"Well, how was *your* day? What have you been up to?" I say in a bright, perky voice, shifting from one foot to the other.

And who the *fuck* is Ludmilla? I want to scream it at him, but I don't want him to know I was eavesdropping. And I'm sure he won't tell me anyway.

"I have been conducting my business, and that's all you need to know." He starts taking off his shirt, which is a little startling.

That's not how we did things before. He would tear off my clothing or make me strip. If he condescended to have sex with me, he'd take off his pants eventually, when he was damn good and ready.

I slide the sleeves of my dress off my shoulders, preparing to step out of it, and he fixes me with a look.

"Did I tell you to take off your clothing?" He sets his shirt, cufflinks and tie down on top of a dresser.

I look at him in confusion. "No. I just thought… What do you want me to do?"

Whenever we walk into this room, I have no idea what's going to happen to me. I only know that no matter how hard and how long he punishes me, and no matter how badly it hurts, I always crave more. The unpredictability of it, the fear pooling in my belly, are a twisted aphrodisiac.

He gestures at the whips on the rack on the wall. "Pick one."

Now, this I'm familiar with.

"You're going to punish me," he says.

Wait, *what?*

NINE

Day two, midday...

"You want me to punish you?" I gasp.

"Do I stutter?"

I take a step back. "Punish you for what?"

"Do you really need to ask?" There's a bite to his tone.

"Well, actually, yes, because you've done so many godawful things to me, I wouldn't even know where to start."

He gives me a grim smile. "You've got me there. Fine. You are punishing me for committing the one unpardonable sin. Hurting children. I did use them as pawns, and it was not fair to them. Understand, they were not abused or frightened or threatened in any way. They wore the finest clothing, and ate the best food, and they had entertainment all day long, and they were tutored during the day. But keeping them from you was wrong."

"So why did you do it?"

There's a flash of impatience in his eyes.

"It doesn't matter. Pick one of the whips, and let's do this."

"I want to know why."

Sergei's brows draw together, and his eyes spark with anger. "Don't presume too much, Willow. I am in command here."

"I know that." But I don't move towards the whips. I am so tired of him shutting me out, I'm willing to run the risk that his mood might turn on a dime.

He stares at me, his gaze burning into mine, and I don't know if seconds or minutes or hours pass, but I refuse to drop my gaze or blink.

Finally, he heaves a disgusted sigh and folds his arms across his broad chest.

"I was afraid that you were breaking down my walls, and I wanted you to stop. I was being an asshole so that you wouldn't try to reach out to me anymore. You were making me look weak. I brought you here to humiliate your family, not take you on long walks in the moonlight." He scowls. "Originally, I planned on sharing you with all of my men."

"You did?" I stared at him in horror.

"Yes." He shakes his head, angry at himself. "No. Not really. From the minute I first saw you at your uncle's house, I wanted you. I manipulated you into offering yourself up as collateral for his debt. And I told myself about all the terrible things I would do to you once you got here, but I never went through with most of them."

"You did enough," I say bitterly.

"Yes."

"Are you going to say you're sorry?"

"That is not something I do, Willow. But I regret dragging your cousins, and Lukas, into this."

Damn the bastard. I want an apology. I deserve an apology. What kind of sick fuck beats up a woman because he's angry with her family?

Then again, what kind of sick loser craves that sick fuck with every cell in her body? What kind of weak, pathetic loser comes back for more, again and again?

Angry, I grab a whip off the wall.

He turns around, and when I see his back, the anger evaporates like a mist and horror washes over me.

I've never looked at his naked back before. Now I realize that there are silvery lines slashing all across it. There isn't an inch of unmarred flesh. There are also scattered circular scars that look too big to be cigarette burns, but could be from a car cigarette lighter or a cigar.

Long ago, someone beat and burned him, again and again and again.

For a moment, I hesitate.

Then I draw back the whip, awkwardly, and slap at his back. At his scars. He doesn't move, doesn't make a sound.

I do it again.

His bored voice taunts me. "I said hit me, not tickle me."

I slash at him again, and he actually laughs at me. "I forgot how weak you are. So weak you can't even keep your family safe. Do you know how easy it was to find you? Your cousins used to cry at night when I brought them here last time, and you didn't even bother to protect them when you left," he sneers.

Even though I know he's provoking me on purpose, rage boils through my veins. I step back and focus on what I'm doing. I go more slowly this time. I make sure that I'm aiming, and I slash at him as hard as I can. When he flinches slightly, I feel a furious satisfaction.

I hit him harder and harder, until he's flinching and grunting in pain with each vicious slash. And it feels good. Too good. All that rage and hurt and fear and frustration that was bottled up inside me – it's roaring through me like a bonfire.

Is this what he feels when he hurts me?

What has he done to me? How can I enjoy inflicting pain on another human being? Defending myself is fine; I have no problem with that. I wouldn't have a problem killing someone if they were a threat to me or my family – but hurting someone for pleasure?

But I don't stop until I'm exhausted, panting for breath. I drop the whip. His back is criss-crossed with angry red weals.

"That wasn't even a tenth of what you actually deserve," I say between gulps of air. I stagger a step backwards and catch myself. Whew. It turns out that whipping someone is a real workout, if you do it right.

"I know."

Then he turns around. His face is flushed, and there are beads of sweat on his forehead. I hate myself for wanting to lick them off.

"My turn," he says.

"Excuse me?" I splutter.

"My turn to punish you. You ran away."

I look at him warily. "You punished me back in the hotel room. Sir," I add quickly, to try to get on his good side.

It doesn't work.

"That?" he scoffs. "That was light foreplay. That was you stalling because you thought you were giving your family a chance to escape."

I shake my head, trying to clear it.

Okay. He just admitted that he knew I was stalling. He's given me a little information. Maybe I can coax him into giving me more.

"How long did you know where we were?" If he tells me, maybe I can figure out what I did wrong.

"You really think I'm going to answer that question?"

I keep pushing for answers. "What ever happened to Jon?"

"I'm sure you know."

There would only be one end for someone who betrayed him. That means he killed him. Brutally.

Jon was a disgusting pig who threatened to rape me, so I'm not shedding too many tears for him, but still...knowing what Sergei is capable of, I feel faintly queasy at the thought of what Jon's death must have been like.

Sergei's gaze is too cool, too controlled.

"You knew he was my uncle's man all along, didn't you?"

A smile twists his lips. "Of course."

"The counterfeit money." It dawns on me. "That was you. My uncle sent real money, and you switched it out. There would have been no reason for my uncle to send counterfeit money."

The look in his eyes confirms it, and I want to cry with frustration.

"I just want to know," I plead. "Did you always know about the apartment in Columbus? Will you please tell me at least that much?" Had he let us all run there and then watched us for two months straight? Because it seems like he knew an awful lot about what we were up to there.

He shook his head. "No, I will not. And now you're about to find out what happens to people who break their agreements with me. You should never have left me, Willow."

Fear blooms inside my heart. His moods can change so quickly. His blue eyes have gone gray now, and his face is twisted into something ugly. He looks really, really angry. It's like he stored away his anger in a vault until it was the right time to use it, and now is that time.

"What if I just apologize?" I say weakly. "For leaving early? Can't I just say I'm sorry?"

"Trust me." He grinds out the words. "You will be sorry."

"But you drove me away. You know that."

He steps towards me, merciless. That look in his eyes…it makes my heart stutter in my chest. "Doesn't matter. You made me a promise. You broke that promise."

"I… I…" I've got nothing.

"Strip," he says coldly, and he doesn't look at me while I shuck my dress, bra, panties and shoes. I leave them in a pile on the floor.

He goes over to a cabinet to fetch his tools of torture. He returns with a string of silvery balls and a bottle of lube. He rubs the silky-soft lube on my rectum, then slides the balls up inside me and does something that makes them start vibrating. It hurts, but the vibration and the burn are strangely erotic.

Then he leads me over to a device that looks likes sort of like a saw-horse, but with the middle board vertical instead of horizontal, with a planed edge sticking upward. There's a chain with cuffs dangling from the ceiling right over the middle of it.

He lifts me and sets me down so I'm straddling it, awkwardly, then chains my hand to the cuffs. I have to stand on my tiptoes if I don't want the sharp edge of the wood to bite into my pussy lips.

"You will stay there for an hour," he says. "If you ask to come off it before then, I'll move on to a punishment that will make you wish you'd never been born."

Oh, like being born with the last name of Toporov hasn't done that already.

And then he goes and fetches a book, and sits down in an armchair, and starts to read. Not even looking at me. I'm dismissed from his mind. And my back is to the only clock on the wall.

I've been working out the entire time I was on the run. At first, I think it will be easy to use my upper body to keep me off that damn edge of wood. After a few minutes, my arms start to ache.

Soon I'm bucking against the sharp edge of the wood. I sink down against it, but if I put my full weight on it, it's agonizing, and I bounce back up. I try to shift, try to get more comfortable, but I can't.

I'm panting with effort.

The vibrating balls distract me and drive me mad. If they were in my pussy, I could come. This is just sheer erotic torture. He's dangling me over the brink, but not letting me have any satisfaction.

The seconds stretch out like elastic. After a while, he glances up at me, his steely blue-gray eyes glinting with malice. "Having fun there, Willow?"

"How long has it been?" I gasp. I've been trying to keep track, counting in my head.

"About thirty seconds."

Panic billows through me. "No it hasn't! You're lying! I counted to at least five hundred, and that was a few minutes ago!"

He shrugs, going back to his book. "Then why ask?" he says, staring at the pages, not me.

"Because it really hurts!"

"That's the point."

I want to scream insults at him, threaten him, beg him…but I'm sure it will just amuse him. It certainly won't make him let me down any faster.

The minutes drag and drag and drag. I sing songs to myself inside my head. I curse myself for not having stronger arms. I bounce up and down, and my pussy is on fire now, and so are my arms. I am gasping and panting. And Sergei doesn't even bother to look up at me.

Finally, I start to cry. Sobs rack my body as I writhe on the wooden torture device. I hate the wood. I hate Sergei. I hate everything. And still he slowly flips the pages of his book.

"Sir, please, it really, really hurts," I sob.

"Yes, I imagine it does." He sets the book down and walks over to me, standing behind me.

He leans in, and I feel his hot breath in my ear. "Do you still think it was a good idea to run away, Willow?"

"No, sir," I cry out.

Calling him "sir" in here feels right. I missed it. I want this. I am desperate for relief from the pain, but this ritual of punishment and pleading...I crave it as much as I hate it.

When he pushes me to my limits, there's a strange kind of ecstasy that fills my body.

He runs his hands over my left butt cheek. "Do you like the Ben Wa balls?"

"No. I hate everything about this. How much more time?" I whimper.

He leans in and bites my shoulder, hard, then licks it.

The sensations of pain and pleasure are too much. I feel as if I'm going to pass out. I want to beg him to let me down, but I'm terrified of him selecting an even worse torture when this one has already weakened me.

"Will you run away from me again, Willow?"

"No!" It comes out as a sob. "Please. Sir. Please, I can't take it! How much more time?"

He licks the curve of my neck and works his way up to my earlobe. He nibbles on it. He cups my breasts with his big hands and squeezes them.

Fuck me. Release me. Let me down.

"You'd better not. Because as bad as this is...it can get worse. Much worse."

His threat should horrify me. It should sicken me. Instead it makes me want him even more. It makes me want to know what "much worse" could be.

His tongue traces the contour of my ear.

"I can last twenty-eight more days," I gasp.

"Are you sure? Right now you're having a hard time lasting an hour," he taunts me.

That's not what I want him to say. I want him to say he'll never let me go, that twenty-eight days won't be enough for him.

Sergei messes up my head like nothing I've ever experienced before. My life used to have rules. They were terrible rules, but at least I knew what they were. Behave a certain way, get a certain result.

With Sergei I never know what's coming. I never know what he'll do next. I have no control over what happens to me.

A wave of dizziness sweeps over me. I can't hold myself up any longer.

I sag, and the wooden edge cuts into the tender flesh of my burning pussy, and I bounce up again with a scream.

"Tell me!" I cry out. "Tell me how much longer!"

"Is that an order?"

"No, sir. I'm begging you, sir."

"Does it hurt, Willow?"

"Yes, sir!" I try to pull myself off the evil, evil wood, and sink back down on it again, and my body shakes with sobs. "Oh, God, sir, I can't... I just can't..."

He smiles pleasantly. As if we were discussing the weather. "One hour. Your time is up."

He releases me, and picks me up in his arms. I'm trembling uncontrollably, and weak as a kitten.

He kisses my sweaty forehead. "Don't leave me again." His tone is harsh, but underneath it I hear an undertone of desperation.

"I won't. I won't. I won't..." I'm shaking and stammering. His arms tighten around me.

He scoops me up and carries me over to the bed in the middle of the room. It's freshly made up with crisp, clean white sheets, and of course it has a headboard and footboard with cuffs attached.

While he's carrying me, I sneak a peek at the clock on the wall. The one that was behind me. It was only forty-five minutes. He let me down early.

That makes me cry harder.

He let me down early. He was merciful.

Everything that he's giving me now is what I craved during those first terrible days in his service. He's told me that he wants me. He's stopped parading me around in front of his men, stopped insulting me and telling me he hates me. He's being as kind as someone like Sergei is capable of being.

The fact that this rough, brutal man is changing for me means so much. But...it's still not enough. He's not asking me to stay.

I force myself back into the present. Nobody can know the future – and that's even more true for me than for most people. I come from a family of criminals who are always waging secret wars. Why worry about what's going to happen a few weeks from now, when I could be dead tomorrow?

He walks away from the bed, and I lie there, shaking, and wait for his return. I reach back behind me and slide the vibrating balls out of my rear channel and drop them on the floor. I hear water running. When he comes back, he's naked – completely naked. So beautiful, he's like an ancient Greek god, a marble statue that just stepped off his pedestal. His cock is rock hard. And he's carrying a tray with a jug of water and two cups of ice.

He pours me a glass of ice water, and I gulp it down greedily.

"Lie down," he says, his voice a gentle caress.

How many Sergei's live inside his head? Minutes ago, he was smiling through my sobs of pain.

But I obey him. I lie flat on my back, exhausted. I close my eyes. The pain and fear fade away, and the only thing that matters is the earth-shattering pleasure I feel as he begins stroking ice cubes across my sore, throbbing pussy.

He bends down to suck my clit, while one hand still slides the ice cubes up and down my heated flesh, and I moan and stroke his close-clipped, silky hair.

He's letting me touch him. My hands aren't bound.

I'm close to exploding. When my breathing speeds up, he draws back, and I let out a shriek of frustration.

"Please, sir," I beg. He likes it when I beg.

"I'll give you a choice," he murmurs. "Where shall I put my cock? Ass, pussy, or mouth."

My pussy is too sore right now. It pulses with agony from the punishment he just dealt out to me. "Mouth," I gasp.

"Then I'm going to make you come first."

He drops the ice. He strokes me with his tongue and his fingers. The pain is receding, just a little. He kisses and soothes, and laps at me as if I'm made of honey. I am pushed closer and closer, until mercifully, I crest and go over the edge of ecstasy, squeezing my legs around his head, weeping with relief as wave after wave crashes over me.

Oh, oh, oh, oh…

He's kneeling on the bed. I get on my hands and knees and take his cock into my mouth. It's so thick, so round, that I can barely accommodate him.

I love his cock. I love the musky taste and smell, so earthy and masculine. I love its thickness, and the salty taste of his pre-cum. I suck it hard. I let it slide down my throat, and I suck and suck as his fingers tangle in my hair and he moans my name. My hand tightens on his shaft, and I move it up and down in rhythm with the bobbing of my head. His moans become wordless, and then he goes rigid and explodes in my mouth. I drink his come eagerly, swallowing it like manna from heaven.

Finally, he slides out of me and pulls me to my feet. I'm so weak he has to hold me up with his arms around my waist.

He draws me up against him. "I have no tender words for you, Willow," he whispers in my ear. "But you do suck cock like an angel."

I manage a shaky laugh. "Coming from you, that's practically a sonnet."

TEN

SERGEI

Day four...

I've avoided her for two days now.

I know she and I aren't a forever thing, and I'm bracing myself for the shock of losing her in twenty-six days.

I'm trying to wean myself from her, like a drug addict. I will only let myself have a little bit of her at a time. I will never let myself get used to the peace I feel when I bask in her sweet presence.

Just having her back under the same roof helps ease the craving a little, but it's not enough.

The frustration's starting to build up inside me, and I know I won't be able to hold out much longer. I should hate her for making me a slave to my desires, but I just can't. God help me, I've tried.

Now I'm leaning back in my leather chair, in my recently repaired office with Jasha, Maks, and Slavik, and they're sitting in a half-circle of chairs facing my desk. Watching me and trying not to let me see that they're watching me.

A week ago, the day before I went bring my Willow home, I was swallowed up by one of my black rages.

It happened when I found out that Vilyat is most likely operating under the name of Cataha in a district east of Leningrad. My men believe that he was involved in the gutting of a young, kidnapped secretary who tried to escape him as he transported her to a brothel. He's managed to bribe the police into looking the other way, though.

I saw the autopsy pictures, the look on her face. There's a particular way that Vilyat guts his enemies and drags their intestines out of them; this matches his M.O. exactly, and the physical description relayed by my spies matches him as well.

I shouldn't have looked at the close-ups. The secretary's face gaped open, her mouth slack, her unseeing eyes a mirror reflecting back the agony of her last moments. She'd been pretty once; you could just barely tell from the picture.

The pictures had slipped from my fingers, drifting noiselessly down to my Oriental rug. I'd destroyed my office. I'd also broken Slavik's nose. That was when I knew I couldn't finish my mission without Willow.

I need her. She's the only thing that holds back the darkness.

My men want reassurance. They want to know that their leader hasn't fallen off the deep end. We're so close now.

We have a list, and we are crossing names off it.

The men on that list are rich and connected, and they aren't easy to get to. And it is vital to us that not a single one of them dies quickly or easily. They all have to know that it is coming, and suffer for months before the horrifying finale.

Humiliation. Terror. Despair. Those are the dishes we force down their throats before they die.

It was the list that inspired us to embark on what seemed like a suicide mission all those years ago – a bunch of street rats starting from nothing and building our own criminal empire in St. Petersburg, Russia. Creating legitimate businesses both to earn money and to hide our less legitimate enterprises.

We were attacked, and every time we struck back ten times as hard, with a viciousness that left no doubt as to the high cost of resistance. Year after year, we forced our way further in. Every last one of us has been shot at one point or another – more than once. We've fought until our bones broke. Our knuckles are studded with thick, knobby scars. Feodyr was run over. Jasha, Maks and I have been stabbed. We've survived car-bombing attempts that scorched and scarred us. A whore on a rival's payroll tried to cut my throat.

None of it even came close to the agonies that we suffered at the hands of the Toporovs and their lackeys. The men on our list.

"Maks, why don't you tell everyone our excellent news?" I say, gesturing at him. He smiles grimly and nods at the other men.

"We're in, all the way," he says. "We will be providing the security."

The other men start cheering, and Jasha hurries over to the liquor cabinet. He starts pouring vodka into glasses. This is truly a cause for celebration!

We've been working on this plan for the better part of a year now. Eliminating competition of all kinds. Bribing or killing officials, whatever it took.

We're building a giant trap to catch a bunch of rodents. The last few names on the list.

One of my shell companies was awarded the construction contract for the rat trap a couple of months ago. We're almost done. It's not fancy or pretty; it doesn't need to be. It serves a purpose. A hideous purpose.

The most important thing about the building is the location. Deep in the forest, in an area far enough out from the city that nobody will accidentally stumble on it. The clients who will use this building demand guarantees of safety and anonymity. We're giving them the illusion of it. Then the trap will snap shut on their vile necks.

As we built the trap, we wove in security systems hidden so cleverly that they'll never be found – until it's too late.

And with us providing the "security" now, we will have complete control over the grand opening.

Willow is back, and the last piece of my plan has fallen into place. It's like she's my good luck charm.

"So soon," Slavik gloats, rubbing his big, meaty paws together. "I'm going to blow up pictures of their faces and jerk off to them."

Maks gives him a scornful look. "Whatever turns you on. Freak."

Slavik cuffs him on the side of the head, hard, but from him, that's a gesture of affection.

Jasha comes back and hands us cut crystal glasses of pure, clear Stoli Elit vodka, and we knock it back, savoring the ice-cold liquid and the taste of revenge.

"Who ever thought we'd come this far?" Maks says happily. "Pour me another, Jasha!"

"What, I'm your bitch now?" Jasha growls, but he complies.

After a few more rounds, the other men head back to work. Jasha stays behind.

"Anastasia asked me if she could go back to her old house to get a few personal mementoes," Jasha says. "We burned all of Vilyat's crap, but we saved her stuff and boxed it up in the garage."

When Vilyat fled the country, I was able to do some behind-the-scenes maneuvering and I got the deed for his house signed over to me.

"Whatever. Go get whatever dumb shit she's asking for and bring it back here."

"I could, but I wouldn't know where to start looking."

I shrug. I'm feeling magnanimous. The people who live in that house work for me. The house was a gift to them, a reward for their excellent service.

"Sure. Watch her every second. Let me know if she tries anything. Obviously, her kids stay here."

"Yes, she says she's fine with that. She said she just wants to get some baby albums and their baby shoes."

I shake my head at the foolishness of women. And at children who grew up with a life like that – with parents who would save a curl of their golden hair, or their tiny little shoes.

Vilyat was an abusive bastard, but fortunately for them, he was a workaholic who wasn't around them that much. His kids grew up drowning in luxuries, and their mother loved them.

As for me? The only reason I didn't starve to death as a baby was because the family next door crept in while my parents were passed out drunk and fed me. They live in comfort now, in a retirement home I bought for them ten years ago, in the Mediterranean. They don't know that it was me who bought it for them. Maybe they suspect. But they haven't questioned their good fortune. They went from living in a tin shack and digging through dumpsters for filthy clothing and rotting food, to living in a warm, sunny seaside condo.

And then my mother miscarried multiple times, because after I was born, her drinking got worse and worse, and my father would punch her in the stomach whenever he found out she was pregnant. Between the alcohol and my father's blows, nothing could grow in that poisoned flesh. She was in jail for slashing the face of one my father's whores for most of the time that she was pregnant with Pyotr. That's the only reason he survived. He would have been better off if he had died like the others.

I was six when she came home with him, and the neighbors had recently moved away, but I was there to care for him. I stole food for him. I stole money to buy him diapers and clothing.

Thinking about Pyotr too much makes black spots swim in front of my eyes, and I shake my head violently to dislodge them. It doesn't work, because they're not real. Jasha looks at me questioningly, with a hint of worry carefully but not completely hidden.

I have to cover. He can't know the truth. He can't know the darkness isn't gone, I've just forced it into a corner of my mind until the last man on our list has gurgled his final breath.

"That's it?" I bark, waving my half-empty glass of vodka at him. As if that's why I'm shaking my head. "What am I, an infant? Why didn't you serve it to me in a baby bottle?" I drain it all in one gulp and thrust it back at him for a refill. He takes it and visibly relaxes. Asshole Sergei, he's used to. It's Crazy Sergei that's making him nervous.

Later that afternoon, Jasha and Anastasia come back from their trip, and he comes to report to me.

"As far as I can tell, she didn't try anything," he says. "She didn't take a purse with her. She was wearing a T-shirt and shorts and sandals, so she wouldn't have been able to hide much, but even so, I searched through everything she brought back. It was all picture albums and baby stuff, like she said. She did ask to use the restroom at one point, and I didn't go in with her, but I patted her down right after she came out, and again when we got back here."

"Her tits? Her crotch? Her ass?"

"What do you think I am, sir?" he snorts. "Soft? Afraid of a little titty? Yes, I patted her down everywhere."

I frown. Something feels a little off.

Anastasia loves her kids. It's not unreasonable to think that she'd want to get all that sentimental crap that women love, all those childhood mementoes. It's not surprising that a woman would need to go pee after a two-hour drive.

And yet.

It could be something, it could be nothing. I'm not sure what I suspect. She certainly couldn't have smuggled any weapons past Jasha.

I can't imagine what Anastasia would fetch from her former home that would be any threat to me, or what she could possibly try to pull. Up until a couple of months ago, she was a drooling, drugged-out husk. She doesn't seem like the type who is capable of making long-term plans. And she knows I'm letting her and the kids go after thirty days. Right now, they're safer than they will be once they leave.

Still, I haven't gotten this far by ignoring my instincts, or by being too trusting.

"Just watch her," I say. "Keep an extra eye on her. Monitor her computer activity especially. She's obsessed with that shit."

He nods, and leaves.

Maks passes him, coming into my office, carrying a laptop.

"Sir?" he says.

"Yes?"

"You need to see what Willow's been searching for on her computer."

He carries over a laptop.

When I see it, fury rises inside me.

Who is Ludmilla? Ludmilla Volkov. Is Ludmilla a common name in Russia? Ludmilla Toporov. Origin of the name Ludmilla. Variations of the name Ludmilla. Ludmila. Ludmylla. Famous women named Ludmilla.

These are some of the search terms that she's been typing in.

"I see." Anger bites into me.

She did this, after I delivered the turquoise jewelry and shoes to her room. She did this knowing that I can see everything that she's searching for online. So she wanted me to see these searches.

Her computer activity has been a concern to me. In Ohio, when she was at her apartment, she used a very effective virtual private network. There are numerous reasons that she could have done that. I understand that she needs to protect herself against her uncles, Vilyat and Edik. Either one of them would snatch up her and Anastasia and the kids for their own revolting purposes. Vilyat would punish his wife for running and taking the kids; he'd torture her to death, he'd sell Willow off to be married or enslaved, and he'd marry his daughter off to someone much sooner than Willow thinks. And sweet little Yuri? Vilyat would beat him to death for not being a cruel, dark monster.

As for Edik, if he got hold of them, he would use all of them against his brother, because Edik knows that Vilyat is the reason I'm destroying their family. He doesn't know why, but he knows that he's lost at least half of his business and has been marked for death. He lives in fear because of something Vilyat did, and for that, he wants to hurt Vilyat and then kill him.

Of course, I plan on ending this long, drawn-out game very soon, but Willow doesn't know that. So maybe she was using the VPN to try to keep track of what her family is up to.

Or maybe she has been spying on me. Maybe that's how she found out Ludmilla's name. How else would she know it?

I send Maks to get her, and have him bring her straight to my office. She's never been here before. I don't mix business with pleasure, but this won't be pleasant.

I am standing by the door when Maks shoves her through it. He slams the door as he leaves her with me.

She's wearing white cotton Palazzo pants and a scoop-neck shirt, and a flower crown headband. My sweet little bohemian angel. I slam the door shut, then smack her on the side of the head so hard she staggers.

"What the fuck do you think you were doing with that search?" I snarl at her. I back her up against the wall. "You think that was funny?"

She goes as pale as a ghost and shrinks in on herself. She's genuinely afraid of me right now. Once upon a time, that would have turned me on. Right now, I feel sick and furious. I don't want to have to beat the shit out of her, but I need to know what she knows.

I grab her throat and squeeze until she wheezes and claws at my hands. "You knew I'd see that search!" I bark at her.

"Yes!" she spits back at me, tears filling her eyes.

I slam her so her head bangs against the wall. "Where did you get the name Ludmilla? Did you hack into my computer?"

She's crying now.

"No! I overheard you talking in the hall the other day! You said that you couldn't wait to kiss her! Or something like that." She glares at me, tears spilling onto her cheeks.

I let go of her, and let out a long, angry breath that I realize I've been holding.

Then I measure out each word carefully, to keep myself from shouting. "I remember exactly what I said. I did not say I couldn't wait to kiss her. I said I could kiss her. That's an expression people use when they are very pleased with something that someone has done."

"Who is she to you?" she screams at me. "Is she your girlfriend?"

I could just slap the shit out of her and tell her it's none of her business. Instead I'm even crueler. I say the one thing I know will break her heart.

"I never told you we were exclusive," I say nastily.

She lets out a screech of pain and rage, and flies at me, trying to claw at my face. God help me, it turns me on so much that my cock leaps to attention, instantly rock hard. She's a magnificent tiger, and her jealousy speaks to her burning passion for me.

I grab her and pin her up against the wall, stretching her arms above her head, shoving my groin against her so she can feel my full, hard length.

She writhes madly, turning me on more. When I lean down to kiss her, she spits in my face.

"Fuck you, you asshole!" she screams at me. "Go kiss your girlfriend!"

I want her right now. I have to have her. The need roars through me, a freight train drowning out sound and reason. But the only way she'll submit to me is if I open up to her. Yet again. I'm giving more and more of myself to her. What will I be when she finishes with me?

"Ludmilla is not my girlfriend, not my mistress," I tell her truthfully. "You're the only one I want to kiss. Or fuck. Honestly, I wish that wasn't true, I wish I could satisfy myself with a whore or a gold-digger, but ever since I've met you, you're the only one that makes my dick hard. In fact, I'm going to bend you over my desk right now and take you up the ass. Do you think you have a choice in the matter?"

Her expression has softened now. Her lips part for me. Her eyes go misty.

I cup her chin in my hand and bend down and kiss her as if I'm drowning and she's my only oxygen. I thrust my tongue into her mouth, caressing the warm silken cave, swallowing her moans of pleasure.

And I don't tell her a secret, one that I think would ruin me.

She's the only woman I've ever kissed on the mouth. In my entire life.

I want to tell her, to make her feel special, because she deserves to feel special and she deserves the truth. But something silences my voice. Something weak and cowardly. I just keep kissing her, drinking her in. She melts into me, pressing herself up against me. Her eagerness turns me on so much I'll come in my pants if I don't get relief.

I spin her around, arm up behind her back, and march her over to my desk.

I bend her over and release her arm. "Pull down your pants for me," I say. She does, with a moan. Her pants fall in a puddle around her ankles.

I kneel behind her and lave her rosebud rectum with my saliva, and slide my fingers in and out of her butthole, moistening it. Stretching it.

Then I stand and push my cock against the tight little hole, and she tenses and cries out.

"Relax," I growl. I move in very slowly, forcing my way up. The resistance of her muscular tunnel makes me want to tear into her like a battering ram, but I listen to her gasps of pain and inch my way in bit by bit, until I'm buried to the hilt. She's quivering, and clutching the edge of my desk so hard her knuckles are white.

She's enduring the pain for me. She gets pleasure from letting me hurt her. God, she's magnificent.

I grab her hips and pump into her slowly. She's whimpering, and I know it hurts and turns her on at the same time. My balls slap against her flesh, and I pump faster and faster, and the hot pleasure builds and builds. I pull out and let go of her hips, and explode, splattering my warm come on the smooth, round globes of her ass. I stand there as the waves of pleasure splash over me, and my panting breath slows to normal.

"Oh," she moans. She turns around, her eyes huge with desire.

I know what she expects. What she craves like oxygen.

She's not getting it. Not today.

"You shouldn't have tried to check up on me," I growl. "So here's your punishment. I'm not going to make you come today. Not only that, but I'm going to come in and handcuff you to your bed tonight, so you can't make yourself come. You're going to tell me before you shower, and I will watch you on the video I have installed in your shower, and I'll jerk off to it, but you're not allowed to touch yourself. I will do this for as long as I want, cuffing you every night, and if you dare to get yourself off before I let you, I will never make you come again. Understand?"

"You... But I..." Tears of frustration fill her eyes. Beautiful, beautiful tears.

"'You, but I,'" I mock her. "Did you actually think that your bad behavior would be without consequence? Get out of my office. Now."

She pulls up her pants and stumbles from the room, gasping.

ELEVEN

Days five, six, seven, eight...

I take great satisfaction in watching her over my video system for the next few days. Her lust for me comes and goes. She tries to act as if everything is okay when she's spending time with her family, but she's distracted and clumsy.

I see how she writhes in her seat sometimes, biting her lip, her forehead creased in frustration. She rocks back and forth. She clenches her fists. She hugs herself. She glares around the room, searching for the hidden cameras that are recording her humiliation. I hold my cock in my hands and jerk myself off until I come, again and again.

Of course, jerking off isn't the same as being with her – but punishing her like this is so satisfying that it's worth it.

God, if only I could keep her. I could spend a lifetime punishing her and then fucking the breath from her body. Devising new tortures to make her moan in pain and weep for the sweet release that only my mouth and cock can give her.

As the days go by, I feel the ghost of something nagging at me, and I revisit our last conversation. I play it back in my head; I have a near-photographic memory.

What I settle on is that she said that she knew about Ludmilla because she was eavesdropping on me. But on the issue of whether she was using the internet to snoop on me or my business…I think she somehow dodged that issue.

I could ask her directly, but she won't tell me the truth.

Instead, I can shake her up just by doing something she wouldn't expect – like taking her out to dinner. That might get her to trust me. To open up to me.

I know that if I offer to take her out to dinner it will be huge for her. So far all I've done is drag her to one room or another and use her for my own needs. I've set the bar pretty low. It's not something I'm proud of.

* * *

Day eight...

I check with Maks for her location, and he directs me to the garden. She's standing in front of her easel near the sugary sands of my private beach, sketching an ocean scene. Her pastels bring the brilliant blue sea to life, and when I look at it, I can feel the water's depth and mystery. She's really good. I feel a welling of misplaced pride when I look at it.

I don't do many good things in my life, and usually when I do, it's purely by accident – I need something, so I do something good for someone to get something in return. But this, I did for Willow because I knew it would be good for her. I encouraged her because I know she loves to draw.

"It's about time you stopped neglecting your talent," I say. "You

99

didn't draw at all after you left here, which was a shame."

She sets down her pastel and gives me a sharp look. "And you know this how, exactly?"

I realize that I've said too much. Now she knows how long I was watching her. I just let information slip, and that is something I never do. And letting her overhear me when I was talking to Ludmilla...what the hell? What is it about her that gets under my skin like this?

Instead of answering, I go on the offensive. I walk over and slide my finger under her chin.

"Willow."

"Yes?"

"To use an American expression, don't push your luck."

She manages a sad smile. "Am I lucky, Sergei?"

"Compared to some, yes." I glance out at the sea.

"This place is beautiful," she sighs.

"My offer still stands. It's yours. You should take it." I can't imagine staying here after I've sent her away. She'd still be here, like a ghost. Every room would echo with her absence.

She frowns. "Prove to me that you didn't buy this place with money from gun running, or drugs."

"Okay," I shrug. "I'll show you the paperwork from my construction company."

She does a double take. "You will? Now?"

"No. No hurry. Maybe tomorrow. Tonight, we're going out to dinner."

Her eyes light up at that. "Really?"

I feel like a bastard. I'm doing this because I want to find out what she's been up to, and she thinks it's a sweet date. Is it, maybe just a little?

"I like you in the blue tulle dress," I say gruffly. "I'll get you at seven p.m."

A few hours later, she's wearing the dress I requested, and she's breathtaking. She doesn't know it. She moves a little awkwardly, and she keeps nervously tucking her hair behind her ear. She's all the more beautiful for her gawkiness.

We drive half an hour to a Mediterranean restaurant, with security in my car, and then another car full of men following behind us. I'm not worried that she'll try to make a break for it – not with her aunt and cousins back at my house.

There are palm trees inside the restaurant, and we're ushered to a room designed to look like a private grotto with frescoes of ancient Rome painted on the walls. There are two other tables there, but my men are sitting at both of them. The single entryway to the room is through a door that only the staff have access to.

A blonde waitress approaches us with the menus and flutters her eyes at me. I glare at her to send her the message to back off.

I order wine for us, and appetizers, and then dinner.

It feels stiff and awkward. I don't do seduction; I never have. I go out to an exclusive nightclub or casino and select the most beautiful whores. If I'm feeling inspired, I take them back to my playroom. When I'm done with them, I send them on their way with a chunk of cash or something sparkly clutched in their greedy little fists.

Willow notices my awkwardness.

"So, you don't take a lot of women out on dates?" she says.

"I don't take any women out on dates."

A startled look flashes across her face. "This can't possibly be the first time you've ever taken a woman out on a date with you."

My lips twist up in a smile. "Not only that, I'm a virgin."

She chokes on a laugh, then shakes her head reprovingly. "No, really."

"On occasion, if it was convenient I might have eaten dinner with a woman. Not on a pre-planned date."

She looks even more confused. "Why would a woman put up with that and come back for more?"

I tear off a piece of bread and drag it through the dish of peppery olive oil. "They don't come back for more. Because I do not invite them. Does anything about me give you the impression that I can offer emotional intimacy?"

"Sometimes," she says without hesitation, which surprises me. She's not lying. "It's hidden deep and it's hard to get to. But when you get to that space..." I see the look of longing on her beautiful face. She wants it to be like that all the time. Or at least more often. If I could give that to anyone, it would be her.

"What about you and your relationship history?" I ask, and then an explosion of rage erupts deep inside me and I instantly say, "Don't answer that." I take a deep breath, clench my fists, and let it out slowly. If she told me about any of her former boyfriends, I couldn't stop myself, even if I wanted to. I'd hunt them down and kill them with my bare hands.

She looks at me steadily. "I have never had romantic feelings for anyone but you. I probably never will again, after you send me away."

"You don't know that."

But I suspect she does. And a horrible part of me is glad. It's not that I want her unhappy. It's just that even after I leave her, I know that I will keep tabs on her, and if anyone got too close to her, I'd cut them to pieces – while they were alive.

Willow is tucking in to her paprika chicken when the waitress comes back, supposedly to see if everything is to our liking. Her gaze drifts over my custom-made suit, my fifty-thousand-dollar watch, my Italian loafers. Women like her know what to look for. A greedy, eager light shines in her eyes.

Her breasts are spilling out of the top of her black halter dress. In Italian, she says, "Too bad you're settling for her. I could show you a really good time." And she gives me an exaggerated wink. I suspect she doesn't realize that I speak fluent Italian, she just thinks she's being clever.

Willow doesn't understand the words, but she gets the gist of it. She stiffens and stares down at the table, humiliated.

I speak to the waitress in Italian. First she smiles, then she goes pale, then she looks at me in horror and flees.

"What did you say to her?" Willow asks me.

I told the waitress that I'd love to take her home with me...because she had such beautiful skin...and I needed a new belt and wallet.

"I'll answer that question if you promise to answer a question for me," I say.

She frowns at that.

"Depends on the question," she says.

I arch an eyebrow at her. "Willow. You hiding something from me, sweetheart?"

She looks at me defiantly. "Why shouldn't I? You're hiding lots of things from me."

"Yes," I say, my voice growing harder. "And it's not a two-way street. I'm the boss here. The master. You are subservient to me."

"For twenty-two more days." There's a quiet sorrow in her voice, and I want to pull her to me, and comfort her, and promise I will keep her forever. I want to give her flowers and diamonds and my heart.

So I lash out. "Why? You want to stay longer?" The old mockery is in my voice, and instantly she shuts down. She shrinks in on herself. She sets her fork down carefully, her meal half finished.

"I'm done."

I should apologize.

I never apologize.

"No, actually, you aren't."

She raises her eyes to meet my gaze, with a quiet, resigned pain. "Well, I no longer feel hungry, and if I eat anything else, I'll probably throw up. If you really want to watch me do that, by all means force me to finish this."

Rage clouds my vision, so I get up and walk away. I call the owner of the restaurant over and talk to him, making my wishes explicitly clear.

A waiter hurries up to us with a carafe of coffee. He sets coffee cups down and pours the coffee for us, and his hands are only shaking slightly, even though he's terrified because he knows who I am and what I can do. Willow is avoiding my gaze. Her shoulders are hunched. She's retreating into that shell that I push her into.

I don't want it to be like this.

I sit down again, and I reach out and stroke her hand. She flinches, as if she'd like to pull away from me and is just barely tolerating my touch. That hurts me on a level I've never experienced before.

"Willow," I say quietly. "Remember that night I went crazy on you? I never know when those moods are going to come on me. You're not safe around me. Nobody is. I'm keeping you here for my own selfish purposes, but when the time comes, I am going to set you free."

"Oh, I see. It's for my own good, then." Her eyes flash angrily. "And in the meantime, you're going to make fun of me and hurt my feelings, to guarantee that I don't try to make you change your mind. Tell me, how well did that work out the last time?"

Fury at her defiance swells inside me like a black tide, and I do something I've never done before.

I push back against the tide. I hold it at bay, long enough to keep myself from exploding in front of her.

"Excuse me," I say to her with perfect calm.

I walk through the restaurant, and out the front door, and across the parking lot to my car. Jasha follows me at a careful distance.

I kick the car several times, so hard I leave dents in the door.

Then I take several deep breaths, and I let them out slowly, and I visualize the blackness flowing out of me like an oily river. I've tried it before, and it's never worked. This time it does. Mostly.

I walk back inside, just as the waiter is setting our desserts down.

She's taking a sip of her coffee, and I sit down and tell her what I said to the waitress. She spews the wine all over her dessert, all over the white table cloth, and goes into a coughing fit that's half shocked laughter.

"You did not," she says to me, eyes huge.

My laughter is harsh. "She disrespected you. So, yes, I did. Do you see her anywhere on the floor?"

She looks around, then shakes her head. "No."

"When I talked to the owner, I had her fired."

She looks as if she's about to protest, then sees the expression on my face – the "don't fucking argue with me" expression – and gives a resigned shrug.

Then she looks down regretfully at her dessert, where she spewed most of her coffee. "I ruined it," she says apologetically.

I push mine towards her. "Here, have mine." At least her appetite is back. I've salvaged the evening.

"So romantic," she says, and then I see a flash of fear in her eyes. "Sorry," she adds quickly. "I wasn't making fun of you."

Arousal flares through me, and guilt. I'm wired wrong. The sight of a frightened woman shouldn't make me as hard as a diamond, but it does.

"It's all right."

I feed her a bite, and she lets out a little moan of pleasure.

I feed her another bite. She moans again and licks the spoon. I watch her pink tongue swirling, lapping up the sweet cream.

"Damn," I say. "I've never been jealous of a dessert before, but I think I'd like to take this tiramisu out back and cut its throat."

She laughs. "Okay, promise you won't get mad at me, but I feel like, for you, that's a genuinely romantic statement."

I start to slip the spoon into her mouth again, then pull it away. She's getting a little too comfortable. I want her to have to work for her pleasure. And she needs that. She wants it.

"Say please," I growl.

"Please. Sir. Please put it in my mouth," she whispers, and a hint of mischief gleams in her eyes.

My cock is about to tear the fabric of my pants, and I'm filled with the strangest emotion, an emotion I can't even name.

I want this. Forever. I want her to look at me like that, with her beautiful blue eyes shining, with just the tiniest hint of fear, because she knows what I'll do to her later.

But men like me don't get forever. There are no happy endings for us.

I let her suck the chocolate off the spoon, and then I lower my voice. "We're done," I say to her.

She looks at me, worried, but doesn't question me.

I call out to my men sitting at the other two tables. "Get out. Lock the door behind you."

My men stop eating instantly and leave the room. They'll guard the door until I tell them otherwise.

"Did you like this dress?" I ask her, and then I tear the neckline with my hands, exposing her small, perfect breasts. Her rosy-pink nipples are pebbled with desire.

She gasps in shock and takes a step back. She shoots a panicked look at the door. We'll have to walk through the restaurant to get to my car.

"When we leave, you're going to be wearing my jacket," I tell her. "Everyone in the restaurant will know why. They'll know what we just did here. They'll know that I own you."

"Oh." Her face flushes with a mixture of embarrassment and arousal.

"Now turn around and bend over the table."

She does, and I lift the hem of her dress.

As I do, I realize that she's distracted me yet again. I think she did, anyway. Is she actually outwitting me at my own game? I wanted to ask her about her web-surfing habits, and somehow I'm about to fuck her blind instead.

I can't stand the thought of her keeping any secrets from me. She's not allowed to keep any part of herself from me; I own all of her.

Tomorrow, I promise myself, I will do whatever it takes to find out what she's hiding, even if it makes her hate me.

Tonight I'm going to make her scream.

TWELVE

I take my tie off and order her to turn around.

"We're in public," she protests weakly, her voice quivering.

Oh, I'm going to fuck her *hard*.

"The room is soundproof," I inform her. I don't tell her that I tested this theory when I killed a man in this room a few months back while diners ate on the other side of the grotto wall, unawares. He tried to sell my secrets to competitors who owned a trucking company – but the competitors secretly worked for me. Nobody heard his screams.

I designed the room the way it is because I am a silent partner, the real owner of the restaurant. It's a good place to lure people who might have their guard up otherwise. After all, what could go wrong in such a public place?

Well, Willow's about to find out the answer to that question.

I bind her hands behind her back.

Then, while I'm still standing behind her, I take one of the napkins from the table and stuff it into her mouth. She squirms and tries to spit it out. I pull out my silk handkerchief and gag her tightly. Now she's making furious sounds, and it makes me laugh out loud.

"What was that, honey? If I want to fuck you up the ass, you're hoping I use lube this time?"

She shakes her head frantically and lets out an enraged squeal.

"Oh, you've been bad? You deserve to be punished?"

I force her to bend over the table. I lift the hem of her dress to her waist, and spank her, hard. She tries to move away. I grab her bound wrists and hold her firmly in place.

Her muffled shrieks just urge me on, and I smack her ass again and again until it's red and glowing, while she writhes and struggles and kicks uselessly at me.

When I slide my fingers between her legs, of course she's wet for me. I massage her pussy, and now she's moaning, spreading her legs wider and arching her ass up. Rubbing herself against me. The spicy scent of her arousal perfumes the air, and I draw it in as if it's my only oxygen.

I make sure not to stroke her too fast, because I don't want her to come before I'm ready. Her squeals of protest have melted into moans of pleasure.

"I'll give you a choice," I say. I love to give her fake choices. "Ass or pussy?"

She desperately struggles to answer me.

Mmmph, mmmph, mmmmph….

"Taking it up the ass hurts, but you know you deserve it? Well, if you insist…" The gag swallows up her cries of protest, and my cock twitches with arousal.

I came prepared. I slide a bottle of lube out of my pocket and I massage her pink, puckered little hole. Then I pull the butt plug out of my pocket and force it in. I slowly slide it halfway out, then back in, again and again, stretching her. I'm in a good mood, so I'm opening her up slowly this time. She's groaning, and her bound hands clench into fists.

She hates it, she loves it…

Finally I slide the butt plug out, drop it on the table, and force myself into her tight rear channel. Her muscles clench so tight that she's almost crushing my cock. She's shuddering, trying to force herself to relax so it won't hurt as much. I pump slowly, and I bend over and reach around, and with every thrust, I stroke her clit.

Her muffled whimpers drive me mad. I make myself go slow. Her head is turned to the side and her cheeks are flushed, and tears are leaking from her eyes. She's pushing herself back, wanting more of me. Greedy girl.

I keep up the pressure on the tight little bud of her clitoris, dragging my finger back and forth, back and forth. She's humming low in her throat, her face contorted with ecstasy.

She's turning liquid with desire. All resistance is gone now. When I feel her start to shudder and clench, I pick up the pace, thrusting harder and harder, rocking the table with each thrust.

We come at the same time, our groans of pleasure mingling, our bodies shaking. The pleasure is so intense it's painful, and the pulses of my orgasm throb throughout my entire body. I stand there, shaking from the aftershocks, until finally they recede and I slide out of her.

When I take the gag out of her mouth, her voice is hoarse.

"You fucking bastard. *That hurt.* And you gagged me!" Willow used to have to force herself to swear in front of me. I loved it. But I love filthy-mouthed Willow just as much.

I laugh at her. "Don't try to tell me you didn't love it."

"Oh, God. I loved it so much." Her words slide out on a moan of surrender. I untie her, and when she stands up, her knees are shaking. I'm still behind her, and I pull her up against me because I glory in making her weak. I love that she needs my strength to stand. We're two parts of a whole right now; her soft core melts my rigid core until I'm almost human again.

We stand that way, and the seconds melt into minutes, and we're the only people in the world. Our island is a nation of two. The pain is gone, the darkness is at bay, and I'm just here, in the present, with no past and no future. This is as close as I'll ever get to heaven.

Finally, reluctantly, I let her go.

* * *

The sun beats down mercilessly on the small clearing in the forest. Vultures are circling overhead. *Cataha's* new men stand with folded arms and scowls stamped on their faces. He actually had to hijack an armored truck to finance the hiring of a new crew. *Him*, reduced to armed robbery. He's better than that.

Cataha looks down at the bodies of the three local police officers. They are sprawled in the grass in the middle of a clearing, their arms and legs flung every which way, puppets with their strings cut. Their mouths gape open, their brains leak into the dirt. A hot breeze carries the stink of excrement; they voided their bowels when they died.

He and his men tortured the police officers for hours, until they were sure that the cops were telling the truth. None of them were behind the leak. They were not responsible for the rescue of those girls.

But they still had to die, because they had done a shit job of looking out for him. He should have been warned that the *Politsiya* were on their way to shut down his operation at the farmhouse. Instead he'd come within minutes of being snatched up and marched off to prison.

So he personally dispatched each of the cops with a shot to the head. One, two, three. The first one stared at him in shock, not believing he was about to die. Then the top of his head came off.

The second and third cried and screamed and begged, their voices shriller than a whore being raped with a hot poker. It was almost enough to make him feel better, but not quite.

He's sure now that his betrayer was the crusading journalist, the one who has declared war on human trafficking in his district. The bastard writes under a pseudonym, Akim. One name only. "Akim" is getting tons of attention, and winning awards and international recognition for *Reforma*. He has gone beyond the duties of a normal journalist. He bribes people for information on *Cataha*'s plans, he slips recording devices into their offices... That's illegal, is what it is!

After the latest cargo was rescued, all the bitches blabbed to the cops and the media, crying loud and long. And so "Akim" caught on to *Cataha*'s latest scheme, and wrote a story exposing the doctor who had helped him select the girls, and now the doctor's life is ruined. *Ruined.* He's on the run, sure to be stripped of his medical license, facing prison if he's caught. It was a sexy story; it ended up splashed on every front page, every radio broadcast, every TV station, all around the world. There's so much heat on *Cataha* right now that it's like standing on the surface of the sun. He's actually going to have to adjust his business model for a while and concentrate on robbery, and he hates that.

The thing about trafficking is, it's incredibly lucrative, but that's not the only reason he's always focused on it as his main moneymaker. He does it because he loves it. He feels like a god when those crying girls are begging him for mercy. It's a rush of power and ecstasy like none other. He has the power of life and death, of pain or relief. And he will be the emperor again.

He mutters curses to himself as he paces. People actually see

Akim as a hero. *Cataha* sees Akim as a show-boating, sanctimonious vigilante asshole, dedicated to ruining successful businessmen like himself.

People see *Cataha* as a monster, but he knows what he really is. He's survival of the fittest. He's a meritocracy. Unlike those weak, undeserving little vaginas who inherit their money or worm their way up through the ranks of the corporation by kissing ass, he fought his way to the top, like a warlord.

He's fortunate that, so far, at least, nobody knows who he really is. He's maintained a front with his new identity as a successful businessman, big enough to live a moderately good life but small enough to avoid attention, and nobody is whispering his real name in connection with *Cataha*.

He's got to take Akim out before he discovers and exposes *Cataha*'s real identity.

Of course, he has to find out who the fucker is first. He's tried to infiltrate *Reforma* to find out Akim's real name, but so far, there's been no joy. They're a bunch of pious little bitches over there, worshipping at the altar of imaginary concepts like "human rights" and "justice".

It's not just the *Politsiya* having a hard-on for him, or the assholes at *Reforma*. His problems are multiplying. The loss of shipment after shipment of girls has created a vacuum, a high demand in the region. Lately, his contacts are telling him that a new player has moved into town, who swears he's offering a solution. He'll be opening up a brothel soon that allegedly has the latest in security technology, and the assurance of protection from the law.

This new, nameless player claims he will have the finest, freshest girls, and he's offering the same kind of anything-goes service that *Cataha* offered in his brothel – before it was raided. Of course, if a girl ends up dead or so severely injured that she has to be put down, the client will have to pay for the privilege, but there will be no other repercussions for the client. Anything goes. In fact, some clients come back again and again, just for that service.

So in addition to plugging the leaks that keep threatening to sink his operation, *Cataha* needs to find out who his new competition is, and kill him.

Then a thought occurs to him.

Maybe instead of killing "Akim" right away, he can use him first. If he can find out the identity of the new competitor, he can inform on the man and take out the competition. *Then* he'll kill Akim. With luck, he'll be able to do it personally, with dull instruments.

The thought brightens his day, and he finally manages a smile.

There's a retching sound, and he looks up to see one of his new crew vomiting into the grass, unable to stand the stink of the dead bodies. Damn. That asshole will have to be replaced.

Good help is so hard to find these days.

THIRTEEN

SERGEI

Day nine...

Temperatures hover in the sixties today, a typical summer morning in this seaside region, only a couple of hours south of Oregon.

Lukas and Yuri wear light jackets as they sit on top of the wooden castle, taking turns looking out over the ocean through the telescope that's mounted there. It's a million-dollar view.

I sit on the patio drinking bitter black coffee and watching them, and can't imagine what they're thinking or feeling. They're like a couple of little aliens beamed down onto my property. Lukas is seven. By the time I was his age I'd shivved a passed-out drunk in an alley so I could roll him and steal his wallet. That was a good take, too. Three hundred twenty-seven rubles, and a cheap watch that I traded for a loaf of bread.

Jasha walks up to me and nods.

"Tomorrow morning," he says.

I smile grimly. "Perfect. I can't wait to see the video."

We're taking out Edik, Vilyat's brother. We already took care of Latvi. And Willow's father, Vasily, died in a highly suspicious plane crash six years ago. I wish I could say I was behind that crash, but I wasn't. I suspect it was one of his competitors. I was still in the process of working my way to the top, in St. Petersburg. I can only hope that he was conscious, and screaming, all the way down, as the plane plummeted from the sky.

We still need to kill Vilyat, but I've been drawing it out. I'm almost reluctant to end it.

Vilyat is one of the last men who was directly involved in Pyotr's death.

Unlike Vilyat, Edik didn't have his filthy little fingers dipped directly into the family business in Russia, but he knew what they were doing. He let it happen.

Ever since we took out his brother Latvi, he knows that he's been living on borrowed time.

His days and nights are agony.

He thinks he's suffering from ulcers, but in fact the chef that I got to has been slowly poisoning him. He used to be a beast of a man who took pleasure in raping women until they bled; we've spiked his food with saltpeter so he can't get it up.

We've deliberately staged failed assassination attempts, and now he's afraid to leave his house. He's terrified, in constant pain, and trusts no one. His wife and teenage sons, who all hate him, have fled to their country home in the Hamptons, and when he ordered them to come home, they refused. He sent an assassin to take his wife out; the assassin disappeared.

Tomorrow morning, we're going to cause a gas main to explode underneath his house. He'll burn alive.

I dismiss Jasha and focus on Willow. I don't like what I'm going to have to do today, but I have no choice. I've stalled long enough.

This morning, Willow used her computer to search on the dark web. She successfully blocked me from seeing what she was looking for. It's time for me to take the gloves off.

Willow, Anastasia, and Helenka are sitting on a bench.

My Willow is wearing a pale green gown as light as gossamer wings, with a cotton shawl thrown across her slender shoulders. I can tell from watching them that they're up to something. Their shoulders are hunched and they're leaning in to talk to each other, talking in hushed voices. They're half smart, half stupid.

Whispering is smart. Surveillance equipment has a hard time picking up whispers. But their body language gives them away. If they just acted normal, they wouldn't be doing anything to raise my suspicion.

I set down my coffee and move quietly through the garden, behind the hedges, until I'm right behind them.

"Willow," I say, and they all jump guiltily.

She glances up at me, startled.

"Oh, hi, Sergei," she says. Her voice is unnaturally pitched, and her gaze meets mine and then slides away. Her obvious attempts at deception give me resolve – resolve I shouldn't need. If Willow were anybody else, I wouldn't even have waited this long. She'd have been strapped to a chair screaming while I snipped off fingers. Nobody lies to me, nobody threatens my life's work and gets away with it.

I paste a look of polite interest on my face. "So, what are you all talking about on this fine morning?"

Willow says, "Nothing that would interest you," at the same time Anastasia says, "Shopping." And Helenka glares out at the ocean, refusing to look at me.

Amateurs.

I smile. "Oh, you'd be surprised. I find a lot of things

interesting."

Willow meets my gaze. "Like Anastasia said. Shopping."

"What about shopping?" I glance at Helenka. "Helenka?"

She scowls at me. "I'm not talking to you, because you're an asswipe, and your douche-water dick-face punks pointed a gun at us and kidnapped us."

"Helenka! Language!" Anastasia gasps.

Helenka's mouth curls in scorn. "As if that's the biggest problem around here." She gets up and walks over to the castle where the boys are playing, and starts climbing.

Anastasia watches her go with dismay. I shake my head in contempt. Oh, how sad, her daughter is turning into a typical spoiled American little princess. Oh, what a nightmare she's living.

When I was thirteen, I slept on a piss-stained old mattress in sub-zero temperatures in a filthy, stinking basement where we shit into buckets. We huddled together for warmth under thin blankets, hands tucked under our armpits. Every morning when we woke up, we'd check to see which of our friends had frozen to death in the night. We'd haul their stiff corpses out into the alleyways. And we'd envy them. Their struggle was over.

I gesture at Willow. "Come with me."

Anastasia looks as if she's about to protest, but Willow quickly holds up her hand. "Anastasia. This is part of the deal. I'll be fine."

No, she won't.

I take her in to the house, to the playroom, and slam the door loudly enough to make her start. The shawl slides off her shoulders and falls to the floor, and she makes no move to pick it up.

I can see the fear in her eyes now. Good.

"Why are you angry with me?"

"What were you guys talking about, really?" I grab her chin and force her to look me in the eye. "What are you looking at online?"

Arousal rushes through me. It's hard to interrogate someone when all you want to do is fuck the breath out of them. When every frightened gasp turns you on.

She just looks at me. She knows better than to lie to my face. Unlike me, she's a terrible liar.

Instead she tries to parry. "Why do you care?" she asks.

"Because obviously you're hiding things from me, which means you are planning something or doing something that you know that I wouldn't like."

Her gaze slides off to the right. "Or you're just paranoid."

"Of course I'm paranoid. Otherwise I'd be dead. But as the saying goes, just because you're paranoid doesn't mean they're not out to get you. You're up to something. Tell me what." I arch an eyebrow. "Or would you like me to ask Anastasia instead?"

"Go ahead," she scoffs.

So she doesn't think Anastasia would break.

She doesn't know what I'm capable of.

"I will, later. In the meantime, I'm not fucking around, Willow. You're here to be useful to me. Not to get in my way. If I think you're getting in my way, then I'll have to rethink my deal with you."

Anger blazes in her beautiful blue eyes. "So your word is no good?"

I tighten my hand, squeezing her chin painfully hard. "My word? Did I give you my word that I would let you undermine me? I don't recall that."

She claws at my hand, so I tighten my grip even more.

"I'm not trying to undermine you!" Her breath is coming out in tearful gasps now.

"Then what are you trying to do?"

She meets my gaze with a mixture of hurt and fury swirling in her eyes. She's definitely hiding something, and it's something that affects me directly.

Anger flares inside me.

I shove her up against the wall and grab her throat, squeezing until her face turns red. I let her struggle for air long enough to genuinely scare her, before I loosen my hands a little. She sucks in a wheezing breath.

"I'm not going to drop it," I say. "And this isn't going to be the fun kind of punishment. When I make you scream, it's not going to be a scream of pleasure. I have plans. I have been working my entire life towards those plans. They are the reason that I wake up in the morning. And you may be threatening them. Last chance to talk."

"Fuck yourself up the ass, Sergei!" And she used to be such a sweet girl – before I got hold of her.

She claws at the backs of my hands, breaking the skin. She tries to knee me in the crotch, and I trap her knee between my legs.

So that's how it's going to be.

That bitter taste in my mouth is back, and I swallow, trying to wash it away. "Let me give you a taste of what you can expect next."

I spin her around and tie her up with her hands yanked high over her head, fixed to a ring on the wall. I adjust her bonds so she's dangling, tiptoes barely touching the floor. The air thickens like molasses, slowing my movements. The sound of her sobs and curses is amplified to a roar in my ears.

I don't want to hurt her.

I will hurt her. It's just one more black mark on my hard anthracite soul.

I grab my bullwhip and I bring it down – hard. She thinks I've been cruel to her before, but I've never genuinely whipped her, not like this.

It snaps across her back, tearing the fabric of her dress, and she screams and her legs dance. There's no pleasure in her scream – it's pure pain and fear. It's a horror-movie scream.

I don't want to keep hurting her like this.

But I do.

I snap the whip again, and she bucks wildly and screams even louder, the sound bouncing off the walls. I feel it vibrating through my body.

"Sergei! No! Please!" she screams at the top of her lungs. Her legs thrash wildly.

And then a third time. Her shriek of pain stabs right through me, and my breakfast rises in my throat. I almost vomit on my own shoes.

Normally when I whip her, it turns me on so much that it's all I can do not to come in my pants. I love it; she loves it. I am the artist of her suffering. I decorate her skin with beautiful bruises which will throb for days before they fade. I mark her as mine. Every time I play with her like that, I can feel her arousal, as if we are one flesh.

Now I am truly beating the shit out of her, and it makes me feel cold and dead and sick inside.

But that is what I am, I remind myself. A thing, not a man. Cold and dead and sick. That's how I deserve to feel.

When we went out to dinner, I let myself pretend that maybe I could make this work, but it was all a pretty lie, a fairy tale I read to myself.

I stroke the braided leather strap on my wrist. I summon up the memory of Pyotr's lifeless blue eyes. That's a dangerous trick, because it can tip me over the edge into madness, but I need that strength now, because I'm about to break. I'm about to let her down. I'm about to go down on my knees crying and begging her to forgive me. I'm about to betray Pyotr yet again – the way I did all those years ago when I let him die.

No. Pyotr, I won't let you down again. I won't let anyone snatch away my revenge – even her.

Sobs rack Willow's body.

I drop the whip, adjust her chains, and spin her around to face me.

She stares at me, horrified. As if she's really seeing me for the first time, and what she sees is a misshapen beast that just clawed its way out of the bowels of hell..

Good.

"Yes," I say, nodding, and I can feel the light of my madness beaming out from my eyes. "This is me. This is what I am. Tell me what the *fuck* you are planning, or I will whip the flesh from your body."

"We're not planning anything!" she sobs. "Please, let me down. Please!"

"Don't make me ask you again." I bend down to pick up the bullwhip.

"All right!" Her chest heaves with sobs. "We've been trying to hack into your computer systems to find out what you're up to. That's it!"

That's *it?*

"What?" I slap her face, and she cries out, her head rocking to the side. Her legs are kicking, desperately, trying to find purchase. She's white with strain.

"What did you find out?"

"Nothing!" she shrieks, but she's avoiding my gaze.

I grab her hair in my hands and start twisting.

"Fuck you!" It's a harpy screech of rage. She'd stab me if she could. She kicks at me with bare feet; her sandals have fallen off.

I grind on, relentless. "I'm one step away from bringing Anastasia in here. I'll take turns between the two of you, with the bullwhip." Sweet, kind Willow. The best way to break her is to threaten someone she loves.

"All right, all right…" She gulps for breath. "I found out one thing. One! And I don't even know what it means. One time, I came across the name 'Operation Salvat'."

"When? And how did you find it?"

Despair twists her features. I've seen that look on the face of those who thought they could oppose me and learned otherwise. I always win. Except right now it doesn't feel like victory.

Her voice is hoarse from crying. "I looked…I looked up what vendors do business with you, and I hacked in to their email accounts. It was one of your suppliers in Russia. But the next day when I tried to get back into their email, I was locked out."

"Ah. That was you." I grab her face in my hand. It's wet with tears. "And what else have you done? Who have you told about this?"

"Nobody!" she stares at me in shock. "Sergei, I'm not trying to betray you! I'm not suicidal, and I wouldn't… I don't want to hurt you."

My cold, hard mask is in place.

"Really? Because I recall a time a couple of months ago when you told me that you wanted to see me go up in a giant bonfire."

"Right after you told me not to come back or you'd kill me?" she shouted. "Right after you said that you'd lied when you told me you cared about me?"

"I didn't say I'd kill you," I say, and I adjust her bonds and lower her to the ground. I free her hands. She slumps back against the wall with a shudder, closing her eyes so she doesn't have to look at the monster right in front of her face.

I believe what she's told me. She could have royally screwed things up for me if she'd succeeded in finding anything, but my security is too good. And she's not actually openly hostile to me. I don't have to do anything worse to her – thank God.

She sinks to her knees, shaking. Too tired to stand. Then she looks up at me, her face twisted with sorrow.

"I wanted to see if I could find any connection between my family and you, because I wanted to know why you hate us so much. I don't care what happens with my uncles – they're evil bastards who deserve anything you do to them, and worse. But I need to know if your plans include my aunt and cousins and me."

"I told you that I'd let you all go when I'm done. That's all you need to know."

She sniffs, hard.

"And I should just believe you because you're such a fine, upstanding citizen?" She spits the words.

"You have no other choice."

"You never leave me any choice!" she screams, her voice hoarse and cracking. "I don't want to just sit there and take whatever you dish out to us! I'm sick of it! I'm sick of everyone else making all of my decisions for me, right down to what I wear!"

"Fine. I'll give an order to burn all your clothes, and you can pick out a new wardrobe."

"It's not that I don't like them! And don't change the subject. You know this has nothing to do with my clothing. I just want to know what the hell is going on here."

Yes, feeling helpless is horrible. I remember it well. I remember what her family did to me, how they snatched away all my choices, and how I prayed for death every single waking minute.

But I don't want her to feel the way I did.

"What does your heart tell you that I plan for you and your family?" I ask her. "Think logically. Your uncle screwed me over, and the smartest thing for me to do would have been to send him the nose off your face. And a videotape of the non-surgical procedure, with before and after pictures."

Her eyelids were drooping with exhaustion. Now they fly open in horror. *"What?"*

That's fine. She keeps trying to love me. She should know what I'm capable of.

"Or I could have sold you and your aunt to a whorehouse, or I could have shared you both with everyone who wanted you. I have done none of those things. I have kept you safe under guard, and I have attended to your every need. You want for nothing. Food, movies, books, beautiful clothing, the free run of this beautiful property. I offered to pay for you to go to graduate school, to support you after I send you away, I offered to give you this *house.* Do you really think that whatever revenge I take will be against you?"

A sigh shudders out of her. "No."

"But if you ever try to hack into my systems or investigate me again, you will leave me no choice but to genuinely hurt you, and every agreement I made with you will be null and void. It doesn't matter whether I want to hurt you or not. I don't. But I can make myself do anything, no matter how horrible, even if it tears my soul to shreds while I'm doing it. To get to where I am today, I've done things that make me sick. You're not safe from me, Willow. Please understand me."

The heartbreak on her face tears into me. "I want to understand you. Part of the reason I was trying to hack into your systems, look into your past, is that I want to know what made you like this."

I look at her blankly. "Why?"

"For selfish reasons. You may not believe this, but I…I love you." The terrible confession rasps out, her throat hoarse from screaming and crying. "Even now. Even after what you just did to me. And I don't want to believe that I would care about a man who is just pure evil. If something happened to you to make you so hard, it would be easier to understand." She looks at me, pleading. "I want to get to know the real you."

"You can't." My words are harsh. Savage. Final.

And that makes her cry. Not tears of pain or fear, but tears of genuine sorrow. She sobs so hard her shoulders heave. I turn to go.

"Don't leave me!" she calls after me.

Every other time she's reached out to me like this, it was like a battering ram, thudding against me, tearing holes in barriers that have been up since as early as I can remember. And I always lashed back at her, mocking her, knocking her off her feet, breaking her heart every time.

I can't do it again.

I walk back to her and I sink down next to her. Without meaning to, I gather her into my arms. She sags against me, her face buried in my shoulder.

I'd die for her. I'd kill for her. I'd destroy anyone who wanted to hurt her – but I can't protect her against her cruelest tormentor – me.

"Why do you want me here?" I ask her gently.

"Because I do. I just do."

She slides her arms around me, and then I'm actually hugging her. Embracing her. Like normal people do.

I gather her up in my arms and carry her through the halls, past servants who quickly avert their eyes, and back to her room. I deposit her gently in an overstuffed armchair. She whimpers in pain from the lash marks on her back.

I'll send a nurse in to take care of her. To clean up my mess.

"Will you come back later and sleep with me tonight?" she asks.

I stroke her cheek. "I wish I could, but I cannot."

Her delicate brows pinch together. "You mentioned that one time a woman slept in bed with you. Why not me?"

She's still jealous. She's insecure because she doesn't know how beautiful she is. She doesn't understand what she's done to me, how she's touched me in places nobody ever has before.

"Do you remember that I also told you that I had a nightmare and broke the woman's jaw?"

She shrugs, unworried about the danger that I pose to her. "I was mostly concentrating on the fact that you slept in the same bed with her." She moves, trying to get comfortable, and grimaces.

"She was a high-end escort. She passed out drunk, and I was too drunk and tired to kick her out at the time."

I see the relief in her eyes.

"Will I ever be able to sleep in the same bed as you?" she asks, her voice so soft, like the caress of an angel's wing.

God, I want that. "I don't know. Probably not. I still have nightmares. I might hurt you."

That last part was a lie, because I haven't had nightmares since she's been back. I hate lying to her. But if I let her sleep with me night after night, I'll never be able to let her go.

"All right." Her voice is small and sad.

For once I want to leave her happy when I go.

I bend down and kiss her shoulder. "Thank you."

"For what?" Her brow creases in bewilderment. Her eyes are watery with tears.

"For being amazing. For loving a monster, even if he can't love you back. For...for letting me see how good it could be, if I were someone else."

FOURTEEN
WILLOW

Day eleven...

I gulp painkillers brought to me by a nurse and huddle in my armchair. I'm wearing clothes that cover the vicious stripes on my back, and I've caked makeup on my face and throat to hide the bruises. I wear long sleeves to conceal the marks of the cuffs on my wrists.

If I move too suddenly, it hurts. I can't even wear a bra right now, because the rub against the wounds on my back is pure agony.

I told Anastasia that I pulled a muscle while I was working out and I'll be lying low for the next few days. She looked at me as if she knew I was lying, but she didn't argue. She just said, "I'll tell Lukas you have a cold." He's been coming around every day now, timidly, with a worried look, afraid to get too close in case I vanish again. He does love to play with Yuri though.

Of course, Sergei hasn't come near me.

I don't know what to think. I don't know what to feel.

I want to hate Sergei, and yet still, no matter how hard I try, I can't. The beating with the bullwhip was vicious and cruel. He choked me until I thought I'd die.

But there's a little treacherous voice inside me, whispering, arguing for him like a lawyer. It tells me that it's my fault. I trespassed into a place I have no right to go. This game he's been playing with my family – to him it's not a game. It's his whole life. His religion, his higher calling. I am the infidel who threatens to tear down the church of his vengeance.

He's a sick man. He's a terrible man. But underneath it all I see glimpses of the moral code that drives him. The way he cares for Lukas, the way he's protecting my aunt and cousins and training them daily to be stronger and safer.

And every time he's brutal to me, afterwards, he opens himself up to me even more. It's almost worth it. No, it's definitely worth it. I'd let him beat me a thousand times, cut my flesh, break my bones...if it would tear away his armor piece by piece, until he'd let me all the way in.

I know what that says about me. It says I'm sick and sad and full of self-loathing. I must be, to want a man like him. But my craving for Sergei is a bonfire that burns away reason. The end of the thirty days is like a date with the executioner.

There's a rap on the door, and I wince. It's got to be one of my family members, because Sergei and his men never knock. I pretend I don't hear it; I want at least a few more days to heal before I see them.

The knocking grows louder.

"Willow, it's me! Are you all right? I need to talk to you!" Anastasia's voice is insistent.

Damn it. What's happening now? Any news is likely to be bad

news.

"I'm here!" I call out. She walks in and comes to sit in the chair next to me. She's wearing a track suit, but it drapes elegantly across her curves. She somehow makes it look like haute couture.

"Jasha just informed me that Edik is dead." Her face twists in a grim smile at that.

I manage a weak grin in response. "Well, thank you for telling me. That makes my day." I shift in my chair and try to hide my grimace of pain.

The Toporov men have been dropping one by one. A couple of months ago my uncle Latvi disappeared, but when police arrived at his house they found so much blood that there was no way he could still be alive. I'd read the horrible details on the news when we were on the run. And I know Sergei was behind it.

"That's...that changes things. So now we only have to worry about Vilyat."

"Vilyat's flying to New York to hold a memorial service day after tomorrow. My guess is, he'll come here next."

Shock ripples through me. I swivel my head to stare at her, my muscles tensing. She looks serene and unworried.

"With Sergei's men on the hunt for him? Why would he risk that?"

She doesn't look anywhere near as worried as she should. "He'll probably surround himself with media because he thinks that will keep him safe. Nobody is going to try anything when the cameras are rolling."

Icy fingers of fear crawl up my spine. Whatever Sergei is planning to do to him, I wish he'd hurry the hell up. God, how much he must hate Vilyat, to have dragged this revenge scenario out for so long. "The cameras won't roll 24/7," I say hopefully. "Surely Vilyat must understand that? And he'll crawl back into his hole once the funeral is over?"

Anastasia gazes out of my window, tucking a golden strand of hair behind her ear. "I expect he thinks he'll be able to accomplish what he needs to, which is to grab the kids and disappear, before Sergei has time to take him out." Her voice is calm and measured as she describes my worst nightmare. And her worst nightmare.

Why isn't she freaking out? She should be freaking out.

"Aren't you worried?"

"No, not at all."

I look at her suspiciously. "Why not? Are you relying on Sergei to protect you?"

She shrugs, brushing the question aside. "Has Helenka talked to you lately?"

"No. I mean, not about anything important. She came to ask me if I felt any better this morning. She brought me some pictures that Lukas drew. She told me that Yuri's working on a death-ray. Why do you ask?"

A shadow crosses Anastasia's beautiful face. "She's just getting quieter. I feel like she's keeping secrets from me, and she never did before. We were a team, us against Vilyat, and now she's pulling away from me." She worries her lower lip with her teeth. "Maybe she's just going through that moody adolescent thing."

"Most girls do, don't they?" I try to reassure her. "In America, anyway? I mean, I didn't, but that's because I grew up with a stone-cold psychopath for a father, and my rebellions were all quiet ones."

My aunt stiffens, and her gaze loses focus. She's staring at something that only she can see. "I wouldn't know a thing about what a normal adolescence looks like." There's an edge to her voice now. "All right, I'm going to rejoin the kids in our daily game of Kick Jasha in the Nuts. I'll see you later."

* * *

SERGEI

Day eleven...

Edik took twenty-four hours to die.

He was burned over ninety percent of his body, and lingered in agony at the hospital before he gasped and wheezed his last breath this morning.

Somewhere, the souls of his victims are surely smiling. Resting a little easier.

Jasha, Maks, Slavik and I gather in my office to drink a toast, as we do every time we cross a name off the list.

Something beeps on Maks' tablet, and he reads a message and then shakes his head.

"That piece of crap!" He spits out the words, his eyes snapping with fury. "Vilyat is coming to the funeral. He's only staying in the U.S. for the day, though, then he's flying right back to Russia, leaving from New York."

Slavik lets out a stream of curses, and kicks a chair so hard he snaps the arm.

I narrow my eyes. "I call bullshit. He hated Edik. He wouldn't risk coming to the U.S. just to play the doting brother, or to spit on his brother's grave for that matter. Step up security until he's gone, and it goes without saying that we need to know where he is and what he's doing at all times."

Maks nods vigorously. "Yes sir. I'm all over that stinking pile of shit."

I shake my head. Vilyat's a fucking moron, and soon he'll be a dead moron. And in a few more weeks, our building in the Russian countryside will be open for business. And the last domino will fall.

My men file out of the room.

I throw myself into my work, so I can stay away from Willow. If I see her in the garden, I stay inside. I eat dinner with my men instead of with her.

When I'm not near her, the pain is with me always, and that's what I deserve. The sharp, steady ache of longing torments me all day and all night, and I revel in it, because I'm an animal who hurt the only woman I've ever cared about.

And worse, she doesn't even hate me for it. I wish she'd hate me. Her love, her loyalty…they're like salt rubbed into my self-inflicted wounds.

* * *

Day thirteen…

Two days later, my men and I gather in my media room to watch the news coverage of Edik's funeral in upstate New York, arranged by his wife. Edik was a wealthy, well-known businessman, and the news of the shocking and tragic accident that took his life is getting a lot of coverage.

Vilyat is surrounded by security, but we catch a few good glimpses of him. I'm happy to see that he looks like shit. He was a vain, handsome man once upon a time, but my terror campaign has chewed away at him. Now he has dark circles under his eyes and his skin is sagging. His hair is thinning. His suit hangs off his diminished body.

On the surface, Edik's funeral is a dark, somber affair. To those who know what's going on behind the scenes, it's a hilarious farce. Every single person there is not just glad, they're overjoyed that Edik is dead. His wife. His kids. His "friends" – all rival mobsters or former co-workers who will move in and take over his territory.

I glance around the room at my men, who are glued to the TV screen. I suddenly realize, for the first time ever, that I'm lucky. If I died, there are people who would miss me and mourn me, fiercely. There are people who would avenge me if I was murdered. I've never stopped to think about that before.

As for Edik? His funeral is a fucking celebration. Everyone's circling, planning on how they'll carve up the pieces of his fallen empire. His wife, with her face stretched into a plastic sheet by too much cosmetic surgery, is chewing her rubbery, inflated lips and glaring at his former business partners, hoping that she'll have something left after the piranhas swim through her finances.

His thuggy kids look sullen and bored. They've worn sweatshirts and jeans to their father's funeral. One of them is violently bobbing his head in time to music on his headphones, the other one is texting.

"Sir," Maks says, an urgent note in his voice, looking at his phone.

"Yes?"

"I just got a message that *Cataha* has been spotted near Pevlovagrad. Today."

A small of explosion of rage flares inside my chest, but I contain it. "You're sure?" I bite the words out.

"Positive. So *Cataha* can't be Vilyat."

I kick the chair in front of me.

"Fuck. Well, I guess he's not our problem, then, unless he tries to interfere with my business."

Jasha makes a sour face. "Odds are that he will. Since he sees us as competition."

I snort at that. Men like *Cataha* don't deserve to draw breath. "I hope he makes a move against us."

But *Cataha* is no longer number one on my list. Vilyat is back in the U.S., and if I can, I'm going to take him out. We've drawn out his torture for well over a year now. We'll strike at the first opportunity.

FIFTEEN

WILLOW

Day fourteen...

Anastasia and I are in the living room, eating a late afternoon snack of crackers, caviar and brie, and sipping red wine from glasses with delicate stems. The children are in Yuri's lab, building model planes. Light pours through the enormous floor-to-ceiling windows and splashes across the tile floor in white rectangles.

I'm reclining on the overstuffed sofa and wearing a cotton cardigan to hide my fading bruises.

My injuries have mostly healed – the outer ones. Inside, I ache more every day. Sergei is making a full-time career of avoiding me, and that hurts worse than any punishment yet, even the bullwhip that cut my flesh open.

It shouldn't have surprised me. If I were smart, I'd just give up hope of finding a cure for the strange sickness that is our relationship. I've tried. I just can't banish him from my heart. And I can't figure out how to hammer through that thick armor of his. What *haven't* I done to get him to love me? I'm out of ideas, and out of hope that it will ever change.

So I'm stuck, waiting at his whim as the days tick off on the calendar, and I hate it.

Slavik is sitting stiffly on a chair, watching us and not saying a word. That man never relaxes. I imagine him sleeping with his eyes open, rigid with rage.

Jasha's across the room, pacing, talking into his earpiece radio. That's not unusual, but something isn't right. His body language gives it away. He's tense and angry, raising his voice now. Slavik gets up and hurries over to him, and listens in.

All of a sudden, Jasha glances our way with a scowl and at the same time I see several security guards running down the hallway towards the front of the house. I set down my wine glass and sit up straight.

Anastasia swigs the rest of her wine before she sets her own glass down.

Then I hear a phone ringing from right next to me - and Anastasia pulls a tiny silver phone out of her pants pocket.

But Sergei confiscated our phones when we got here. And I've never seen that phone before. Where the hell did she get it?

Alarm stabs through me. It won't be long before they notice Anastasia's phone and she suffers whatever consequences Sergei decides.

For the moment Jasha's distracted, shouting into his radio now, in Russian. "Tell the reporters to get the fuck off our property or we'll call the police."

My wine and cheese curdles in my belly and almost comes back up. Reporters are here? That almost certainly means Vilyat is here. That's his thing these days.

Anastasia is serenely calm, smiling. There's an inner glow to her.

I stare at her. "You've got something up your sleeve." Hope blossoms. "Please tell me it's something good."

Her pink lips curl up in a small, secret smile. "It's very good. It's the answer to all our prayers. I have freed us all." There's a note of quiet pride in her voice.

I look at her askance. Does she know what she's doing? What does freedom mean for us, these days? We need Sergei's protection. Yes, he's holding us prisoner, but he is most definitely the lesser of two evils. Just getting out the door alive isn't our goal. We'd run right into Vilyat's arms.

Sergei storms into the room, barreling towards us with murder in his eyes, and I flinch, but then I brace myself. He's hurt me before. Whatever he does to me, I can survive.

And I'm mad as hell that he's been avoiding me.

"Nice to see you again," I snap.

He flicks me a quick, chilling glance. "Now is not the fucking time, Willow."

Anastasia ignores us, lips pressed against the phone, speaking in low, urgent tones. "Yes, I'm ready," she says.

She looks up at Sergei, the phone hovering inches from her mouth. "My lawyers are outside. Open the front gate and let them in. And the reporters. And my piece of shit husband."

Sergei makes to grab for the phone, but she rears back. "I'm still on the phone. My lawyers are listening. Touch me, and I'll scream for the police."

He freezes in place, and I swear I feel the temperature around us drop by a couple of degrees. The hair stands up on my arms, and goose pimples ripple over my skin. Has Sergei just sucked the heat from the air, or am I simply that terrified?

"You really don't want to pull this right now, Anastasia," he says, in a low, furious voice. "Your husband is out front, telling the news cameras that he's here to file for custody of his kids and saying that they're being held prisoner."

Anastasia arches her delicate golden brows. "Well, he's not lying."

I can feel the rage rippling off Sergei's skin. It makes the air hot and prickly and painful. "Have you thought about what would happen if you leave here with your kids? If you no longer have my protection?"

"I have."

Sergei holds out his hand for the phone. "Last chance."

Anastasia leaps to her feet, taking several steps back. *"Let them in."*

Sergei growls in rage. Then he snaps at Slavik. "Give the order. Let them in."

"But… All right." Slavik pulls a radio from his pocket and barks into it in Russian, and the look that he's giving Anastasia is so sharp I'm surprised she's not bleeding.

Anastasia hurries towards the foyer, with a furious Jasha trailing at her heels. I see Helenka in the doorway of the living room, waving at me frantically, so I go to her. Slavik heads towards us, hovering like an avenging angel.

"What the hell is going on?" Helenka demands, her face pinched with that look of sullen defiance she wears so often these days. I don't even bother to chide her for her language.

"Damned if I know. There's a bunch of reporters outside, and your father is out front saying he's filing for custody, and your mother somehow smuggled in a phone and called lawyers, who she's about to meet with right now."

Slavik is mumbling curses under his breath.

"Well, that's more than my mother told me! She won't tell me *anything*," she says furiously. "I'm not a damn child. I have a right to know if my sperm donor's trying to kidnap us." Then oddly, unexpectedly, she throws her arms around me and hugs me. She's never been much of a hugger. I try not to wince openly; my back is still sore.

I hug her back, awkwardly. She stands on her tiptoes and whispers into my ear "My mother's password is Z7352KP." She repeats it, in a whispery sing-song. "Z7352KP, Z7352KP." Slavik is trying to listen to something on his radio, but he looks up and glares as Helenka is embracing me.

"Oh, excuse me, you have a problem with this?" I snap, going on the offensive. "This is called hugging. It's what humans do."

"You know what else humans do? They bleed when they're shot," Slavik growls.

"Blow it out your ass." I can't believe Helenka's delicate little mouth just spewed those words.

That's it. "*Language!*" I say indignantly.

"English is my preference." She smiles, a glint of the old mischief in her eyes, and releases me.

I casually slide my hand into my pockets. She's slipped an envelope into the left one. Clever girl.

"Your father's coming into the house. Go find Yuri and stay with him," I tell her. "I think he's in the robot room. We won't let your father take you. If it comes to that, I'll stab him and do the prison time before I let that happen. I'm not kidding."

"No, no," Helenka protests. "*I'll* stab him. They'd just send me to juvie and I'd be out in no time." She hurries off to find her brother. I groan and palm my face. The fact that she's actually thought this through is really messed up.

I swallow hard and stalk off towards the foyer. Slavik and Sergei are there, and they both move to block me. Sergei's face is flushed with fury, and maybe I'll be scared later, but right now I'm so stunned that I'm floating in a helium balloon, above it all.

"Move, or I'll scream my lungs out," I say. I can hear voices in the foyer, so I know that the lawyers are there, and they'll hear me if I scream.

Good Sergei is gone. His eyes have turned that terrifying color of hard steel that promises to slice flesh from bone, and his soft, sensual lips have thinned to a hard line. He doesn't say a word to me. He doesn't have to.

"I am going to fuck you up for this," Slavik snarls at me, stepping out of my way. Sergei doesn't move.

"It's a date, then," I say to Slavik with sweet sarcasm, and I dodge around Sergei and hurry to the foyer. Slavik and Sergei are right on my heels.

In the foyer, Anastasia is huddled with four men in suits. How did she get hold of them in the first place? How could she pay them?

Jasha is hovering next to them, a look of helpless rage on his face. The front door is open, and outside on the front steps, I can see the news cameras and the clustered horde of reporters.

I pray that Anastasia's plan involves more than lawyers. Lawyers won't be enough to keep her kids safe from their father.

I turn on Sergei. "This is your fault," I say, in a low, angry voice. "You dragged this out way too long. You should have taken care of Vilyat months ago, and now there's a real chance he's going to be able to take the kids and flee the country."

"Like I give a fuck what happens to them," he spits at me.

That shouldn't hurt me, but it does. I can't let Sergei be pure evil. My heart won't accept that. "You do. I know you do." I'm pleading with him now, my earlier defiance leaking away. "You said it yourself. You don't hurt children. You're telling me it's okay if someone else does?"

Before he can spit out some answer that will stab me to the core,

Vilyat pushes his way forward through the crowd with two big, bulky bodyguards. "Let me see my children!" he shouts at the top of his lungs, playing up to the news cameras. "I am their father! You can't keep them from me!"

One of Anastasia's lawyers steps forward and holds up a computer tablet. He thrusts it at Vilyat's face, and the result is astounding. Vilyat's face flames red, and he staggers back a step. Anastasia doesn't look the least bit afraid. How can she not be afraid? I want to pee my pants.

Suddenly, Vilyat goes insane with rage. He punches the lawyer in the nose, sending him staggering, and blood sprays everywhere – right there in front of the news cameras. The lawyer cries out, clutching his face.

Vilyat lunges for Anastasia, and his hands close on her throat. "Bitch! Cunt! I'll kill you, I'll fucking kill you!" he shrieks.

Live on camera.

Jasha rushes forward and punches Vilyat so hard that Vilyat goes flying backwards into the arms of his bodyguards. Anastasia drops to her knees, clutching her throat, gasping and wheezing. I can tell that she's putting on a performance, but it's an excellent one. The cameras are eating it up.

Jasha goes to help her stand up, and she tries, but falls to her knees again.

Damn, she's a good actress.

He's kneeling next to her, patting her back.

There must be twenty news cameras on Vilyat as his men hold him back.

Anastasia staggers to her feet, clutching Jasha for support, and turns to face the camera. "That's what I've lived with for the last fourteen years!" she cries out. "This man, he pretends to be a philanthropist, but it's all lies. He just showed you his true face! He beats me and he beats my children. He has broken my bones. He has left scars on me that will never fade. That is why I am filing for divorce today."

Flashbulbs pop, reporters shout questions and jostle for position, eager to get the best shot or video clip of the wonderful story spooling out in front of them.

Vilyat's fighting with his bodyguards, kicking and screaming, swearing in Russian and English. One of the lawyers slaps a piece of paper against his chest. "You've been served," he says, loudly and dramatically, playing to the cameras. The paper falls to the ground, but it doesn't matter. Legally, he's been served.

And my heart sinks. This is her grand plan?

"Oh, no," I whisper to Sergei. "It's not enough." He can bury her under a mountain of lawyers, he can bring up her abuse of prescription drugs... If Vilyat goes to court for a custody battle, he may very well win. Or he'll be forced to take some bullshit "anger management" course and then he'll be given unsupervised visitation with the kids, and they'll all disappear.

And if Vilyat is careful enough, he may even be able to avoid Sergei's hit men while he's doing it. It will be much harder for Sergei to take him out with all this publicity.

"Yes," Sergei says nastily. "I could have told you that. This will never work. She's screwed herself up the ass without lube."

Anastasia looks at Vilyat, who's panting for breath now, eyes wild, hair disheveled.

"You will apologize," she says loudly. "Not just for now, but for abusing me and my children over the years."

One of the lawyers is holding the tablet up to his chest, and he taps it significantly.

Vilyat sucks in a deep, shuddering breath, and he looks like a giant, evil baby who's been disciplined and wants to tantrum but doesn't want to be spanked.

There is something on that tablet. Something good. Or rather, something terrible – something that Anastasia is counting on to protect her from Vilyat. Now I'm starting to feel hopeful again. Maybe Anastasia really can pull this off.

Vilyat looks at the cameras. The reporters are rapt, enthralled.

"I am sorry for anything I may have done to upset my wife, who I love very much," he grits out. "Of course, I am under an enormous amount of strain today, having just buried my dear brother." Fucking little weasel, trying to lie and diminish what he's done to her.

She's not having any of it.

"What *upset* me was you kicking me in the ribs and breaking my bones!" she yells at him. "Do you remember doing that?"

Vilyat looks as if he's about to have a stroke. "Yes. I remember."

"Do you admit to abusing me and your children? Hitting us with your fists? Kicking us? Threatening us?"

The lawyer taps the tablet again.

Sweat pours down Vilyat's face. He shuts his eyes, shaking, his fists clenched. It's remarkable. It's wonderful. We're watching the devil tear himself apart inside. "Yes. I admit it. I am sorry that I lost my temper."

The reporters are shouting at him. "Vilyat, why did you beat your wife and kids?"

"Vilyat, did you really hurt your children?"

He's shaking, struggling to control himself.

Anastasia's eyes glow with a crazy, malicious light. "I *believe* that what you want to say is that you are sorry you have been abusing me and the children all these years."

He grimaces as if he's just swallowed poison. He sucks in a breath. "Yes. I am sorry about that." His dark eyes glitter with hate as he bites out the foul-tasting words. "Of course, I will strive to do better, and I will do anything to make my family whole again."

Anastasia looks at the cameras. "That will not happen. This man broke my bones and slapped my son so hard he ruptured his eardrum." Ugh. I never knew that. "I am filing for full custody of the children, and I expect to terminate his parental rights."

The reporters push forward, and they're shouting questions at her, but Jasha helps her stumble back inside the house, with her lawyers crowding around her. The door slams shut, so they follow Vilyat instead. I peer out through a window and see them surrounding him, and he's furiously shoving at them and throwing punches.

SIXTEEN

WILLOW

Day fourteen...

Hope and hysteria bubble up inside me as I hurry to my room. I reach into my pocket and pull out the envelope Helenka slipped in there. Inside the envelope is a thumb drive.

I plop down in my chair, turn on my laptop, and plug in the thumb drive, and the screen goes black, asking for a password. I give it the password that Helenka gave me.

I don't have much time. Maks will be monitoring my computer activity, and whatever I see on here, he'll see too.

A grainy video starts playing, and I almost fall off my chair.

There's a woman tied hand and foot to a bed, thrashing, screaming in agony. A man is grinning and pressing a hot branding iron to her stomach. He's an older man with a big shock of white hair, and he looks vaguely familiar. I think he's a famous Russian politician, I just don't remember which one.

He presses the branding iron down again, and she makes sounds that aren't even human. Wordless howls bubble up from her throat, and then her eyes roll up in her head, and mercifully she passes out. But she isn't out for long. Someone hurries over and zaps her with a cattle prod, and she convulses and gives a strangled cry.

I back away from the computer. I can hear her screaming and pleading. I clap my hands over my ears.

Please, no, please kill me, no, I'm sorry, no....

I hear footsteps pounding down the hallway, and the door flies open. Sergei, Maks and Slavik storm in.

Maks grabs the laptop from me. "Give that back!" I cry.

He spits out a contemptuous laugh and looks at the screen. His face wrinkles in disgust at the scene being played out there. Sergei's mouth twists and his brow furrows, but he stares straight at the screen without blinking.

Then Maks sets the laptop down. I can hear the man shouting insults at the woman he's torturing, mocking her. What hell-pit spawned him? What makes a man into a demon?

"Hey! You! It's demanding a password," Maks says impatiently. I look. A box has popped up on the screen now, although the nightmare scene is still playing. The man pushes the branding iron down onto her breast, and she screams so hard she chokes, eyes bulging. "What is the password?'

Shaking, I repeat the password. He tries it – and the screams stop, and the screen goes blank.

"No!" I cry out. "That was the password, I know it was!"

Maks shakes his head, frantically pushing keys on the keyboard, but the computer isn't responding at all now. The screen is black as night.

"This needs to be given to the police," I say desperately. "Get the video back up! Fix it!"

"There's a virus destroying the computer as we speak," he says.

"There would be nothing to give them but a fried hunk of metal."

Anastasia and her damn computer security lessons. She's thought of everything.

Slavik hears something on his earpiece radio. He nods to Sergei, and all the men hurry out of the room.

As Sergei is about to leave, he says, "Don't try to leave this room, or I will end you. I'm not fucking around." He locks the door behind him. I hurry over to the glass door that leads out to the garden and try it; it's locked. It's never been locked before.

I pick up a chair and swing it at the glass – and it bounces off. Shatterproof glass. Of course. Not only that, but I see a little red dot winking in one of the curly wooden rosettes that adorn the doorframe. A security device. Now Sergei will know I tried to break the glass.

I don't care. Anastasia knows something about that woman being tortured, and I need answers. The woman is almost certainly dead, but this must be somehow related to Vilyat. She's gathered information about him and given it to her lawyers to use as leverage. She surely must have enough to take him down, to expose him, and the man with the white hair, and probably others.

They're only gone for about ten minutes before Sergei comes back to fetch me. "Your aunt wishes to speak to you," he says, his voice wooden. The steel is still there in his eyes, and I shiver.

He walks away without looking back, and I hurry after him. His legs are much longer than mine and they eat up the distance with fast, furious strides. I practically have to run to keep up with him.

Anastasia, Helenka and Yuri are gathered in the foyer. The lawyers are surrounding them, shielding them, including the one whose nose was punched. He's got a bloodied napkin wadded up and pressed against it.

I wave at Anastasia. "I need to talk to you privately, now," I snap.

She frowns. "Willow, we're all leaving together. Talk to me while we're driving."

"Nope. Give me two minutes."

Anastasia hurries over to me with a hiss of exasperation. Sergei is standing behind me, burning the oxygen from the air with his rage.

"What is it?" Anastasia demands impatiently. "Come on, Willow, I want to get out of here. Sergei has agreed to let us all go and leave us alone completely." Like he had a choice.

"Helenka gave me a thumb drive with a video of a man torturing a woman," I say. "And now it's disappeared from my computer."

"She what?" Anastasia sucks in a gasp of dismay, and glances at Helenka, who is leaning to the side, peering out from behind one of the lawyers. Helenka shoots her a look of angry defiance. Anastasia leans in to me, lowering her voice. "She didn't see the video, did she?"

"I'm pretty sure she didn't. Since Sergei only let you and me have laptops, she probably didn't get a chance to watch it. She told me she's upset because you're keeping secrets from her."

"Of course I am!" she whispers. "If she knew everything her father did, it would destroy her."

"She's stronger than you think. Obviously this video needs to go to the police and Interpol. Along with everything else you've got on Vilyat. The video disappeared. How do I get it back? You must have copies?"

"I have the information stored where it's safe. And you can't have it."

I look at her in horror. "Anastasia. The police need that information."

She shakes her head. "No. I have forced Vilyat to agree to a divorce, and he's going to let me terminate his parental rights. He's also giving me two million dollars which will be in an offshore account by the end of the day, and paying my lawyers an additional two million. He knows that if I die or disappear, everything that I have on him will be made public. I need this information to hold over his head. If I take it to the police, he might be able to beat the rap. Or he might get out on bail, kidnap the kids, and flee the country."

Anguish floods through me. "You… I mean… Where did you get all of this information?" Maybe I could retrace her steps. Find out where she got it, get it myself, destroy him…

She waves her hand in dismissal. The kids are staring at her, their eyes as big as saucers. She glances at them, then shakes her head impatiently. "It doesn't matter. I've been gathering it for years, waiting for the right time. Vilyat got comfortable and sloppy around me, and let his guard down. I've always been good with computers, even before I started taking those online classes, I just didn't let on before now."

Sergei burns her with his contemptuous gaze. "You had the information hidden in the bathroom of your house. That's why you went back there. You shoved it up your twat to smuggle it out. Along with the cell phone, I'd imagine. Hope it wasn't too uncomfortable."

"After all the things Vilyat has forced inside me, that was probably the least painful thing I've had up there," Anastasia sneers at him.

I feel sick with disgust. There are women being tortured right now, and Anastasia won't help them?

"Sergei. We've got to get that video back," I plead.

He shakes his head. "We can't. Maks is the best, and if he can't get it back, it's gone. It self-destructed when we couldn't give it the second password. I will be taking care of Vilyat soon enough, and that's my only concern."

"No, it isn't! That woman in the video, Sergei, you saw that!" I cry, tears burning my eyes. "If you don't care about that, you aren't human! And don't give me that melodramatic bullcrap about how I already knew you're a monster, blah blah blah. That is a completely innocent victim being tortured."

There's no pity in his gaze. How is that possible? "She's dead by now. You must realize that."

"But the men who did that to her aren't, and they'll do it again!"

"Well, Vilyat won't. Because I'm going to fucking kill him." His face is a pitiless mask.

Helenka and Yuri are watching us from the foyer, horrified, fascinated.

"Keep your voice down," Anastasia snarls. "There is no need to drag them in to this."

"Sergei," I plead, ignoring her.

He won't be moved. "The laptop is fried. If we go to the police, I'm sure your aunt will just lie about it. We've got nothing."

I swing around to face my aunt, and I shove her, so hard she staggers. I've never laid my hands on her before. "Anastasia," I rage. "You fucking *bitch*. The women out there, the current or future victims, those are someone's children too. I swear to God, if you don't go to the police, I will find a way to bring you down."

Her face goes slack. Her eyes are blank empty pools of despair.

"How old am I?" she asks.

I shake my head in confusion.

"What the hell does that have to do with anything? In your thirties. Who cares?"

"I'm twenty-five."

She's trying to claim that she is three years older than me? Twenty-five with a thirteen-year-old daughter?

"No. You were eighteen when you married Vilyat."

"No, I was not. I had just turned twelve. He came to the child whorehouse that he ran with your father, the one for little girls. There was also one for little boys, by the way. And I'd be willing to bet my left tit that Sergei was in one of those boy whorehouses at some point. He's the right age; the math adds up. What else would make him hate our family so much?"

Sergei doesn't move. I don't think he's breathing.

No. Fucking no.

Anastasia won't stop. She keeps stabbing my heart and mind with her words. "When Vilyat came to the whorehouse, I knew he was one of the owners, and I made him notice me. I managed to convince him to take me, to marry me, by pretending to be a frightened little virgin. I wasn't a virgin, of course, but I used fake blood. I'd been pimped out since I was nine. I ran away from my pimp, and after a few weeks of living on the street on my own, your father's men caught me and dragging me screaming into a truck, and they beat me bloody for screaming, and took me to the whorehouse."

I'm splintering into a thousand pieces.

Anastasia's voice is coming from somewhere up in the stratosphere now, hollow and echoing. "Helenka and Yuri have choices. They can choose their outfit, their breakfast, their boyfriend or girlfriend, their career. When I was their age, I had choices too. Convince a pervert to rescue me by seducing him with my fake cherry, or stay there and let old men rape me until I died. I thought Vilyat was a good catch, back then. He was handsome. He wasn't old like the others. God, was I sick of sucking wrinkled old cock." She shudders in revulsion at the memory.

I feel so cold and alone, as if I'm floating away on an ice floe.

Could this be true? Was my father a child-raping pimp?

"How old was my mother when she married my father?" My voice is a husky whisper.

Twenty. Please say twenty. That is what she told me. It must be true.

Let me keep something.

She sighs, rubbing her hand across her beautiful face. "Fifteen."

I can hardly feel my own body, but I summon up the last of my strength from somewhere and look at her. Tears are pouring down my face now. "Anastasia, women like Helenka are being raped right now. Young women. Little girls. Go to the police. I am begging you."

She scowls at me.

"The police force there is riddled with corruption, and the men who use Vilyat's services are rich and powerful. How well do you think that would go?"

I can't give up. I must fight for those women. If I were one of them, I'd want someone fighting for me. "I've been reading in the news about the *Politsiya* raiding brothels in the St. Petersburg area over the last couple of months. Shutting them down, saving the women, arresting lots of people. Including politicians and a judge. So not all the cops are corrupt."

She shakes her head wildly, blonde locks flying. "Enough of them are. My first client? A cop. Do you know how much cop semen I swallowed before I turned ten years old?"

I taste vomit in my throat, but I won't give up. "Obviously if Vilyat is so afraid of what you've got on him, you have useful information."

She takes a couple of steps backward. Now her tone turns sharp and nasty; her eyes snap with resentment. "It's easy for you to be self-righteous, Willow. Your mother kept you safe. Your father saved most of his abuse for his whores." *Another blow.* "You've never experienced what I have. I pray you never will. But I am going to do whatever it takes to keep my own children safe, and frankly, everybody else can just fuck right off. You think those women would risk anything for me? The world is an ugly place, Willow, and people only look out for their own."

My breakfast is rising in my throat. "Then go. I'm staying here. I don't care what they do to me. And you? You're dead to me."

She turns and walks away, and Yuri start crying when they realize I'm not going too. Helenka throws a final glance back over her shoulder, her eyes haunted. The lawyers hustle them out the front door, and they're gone from my life.

Jasha watches the door slam, and then tears his gaze away. I can see that he doesn't want her to go. I don't think he deliberately betrayed Sergei, but I think that he was slack in his surveillance of Anastasia because he was developing feelings for her. She probably knows that, and she doesn't care about him any more than she cares about me, or those women who are dead or dying, or anyone besides her kids.

I look at Sergei with drowning eyes.

My life was a lie. My mother was a child bride. The blood of monsters runs through my veins.

His face is grim, impassive.

"Tell me about my family. Tell me what they did to you. Tell me!" I scream.

"I can't."

Rage flares inside me. I've never felt anything like it. It consumes me like a wildfire. I turn and run into the living room and grab one of the empty wine glasses, and smash the cup off it. I slash my arm with the stem, drawing a bright red line of pain through my skin.

Sergei and Jasha pound towards me. I swing to face them, waving the glass stem, wild eyed, and then I jam the stem up against the tender flesh under my chin.

"Fucking tell me," I scream. "My only family that I care about is leaving here, and I will probably never see them again. They're safe, so you know what? I have no reason to keep myself safe anymore. What are you going to threaten me with? Pain? I'll cut my own throat,

Sergei, I swear to God I will."

Jasha lunges at me and snatches the glass away.

My bones turn liquid and I fall to the ground, screaming and crying. "Tell me. Tell me. Tell me. Tell me."

Then I realize that I'm in Sergei's arms, and my throat is raw. I'm staring up at the ceiling, heaving. How long have I been screaming?

"Please." I've never begged like this before. "If you don't tell me, it will kill me. Nothing you can tell me will be worse than what my mind will fill in. For the love of God, I've got to know. The pictures in my head right now – they're killing me."

Sergei bends down and oh so gently kisses my forehead. Right there in front of his men.

He strokes my hair, and his eyes plead with me. "Willow. You're too good for this. Too pure. It will poison you."

"It's already too late."

"Fucking Anastasia," he curses furiously.

I choke on a sob. "Oh, for God's sake, Sergei. Yes, what she's doing is wrong, but she's a feral animal protecting her young. If I'd been raised like her, I might do the same thing. If you don't tell me…it will end myself, one way or another."

He stares at me, his gaze tender and infinitely sad.

"If I'm going to tell you about it, we need to make some preparations," he says. He glances up at his men.

Maks pulls me to my feet and sits me down on the sofa, while the rest of them leave. "Stay there," he grows at me. I couldn't move if I wanted to. I am weak with fear of what I'm about to find out.

He comes back with a first aid kit, a towel, and a bowl of water. He washes and bandages my arm, without looking at me.

Then he leads me through the mansion until we reach a room. A padded room.

Sergei is inside, and I stumble in, shaking, even though it's not cold.

"Stand right by the door, and be ready to run," he tells me. He glances at Maks and Jasha and Slavik. "Take her out if I get too…"

"Yes," Jasha says with a grim nod.

"And don't leave her alone for a minute. She's on suicide watch. When she goes to the bathroom, the door stays open."

"Of course." Jasha's voice is weary and resigned.

Sergei runs his fingers through his hair, and his eyes go vacant as he stares into space. Into his past.

"Let me tell you a story," he says.

SEVENTEEN

SERGEI

"I already told you a little bit about my parents, but I didn't give you the full story. They were drunks and monsters. We were dirt poor, and they spent every kopek on alcohol. I only kept Pyotr alive by stealing food for him. I did everything I could to keep the harshness of the streets from him.

He was a sweet little boy. When we were next to starving, I was feeding him and he wasn't gaining any weight. I found out why. He was giving half his food to a stray cat who'd just had kittens. I was furious – I wanted to kill them all – but he cried and begged, so I relented.

He appreciated every single thing I gave him. I would steal a toy for him, and bring it home. I'd never tell him that, of course. He would have refused to accept a stolen toy.

Whatever I gave him, no matter how small or shabby, he'd light up like a Christmas tree. He was so excited and so grateful. That was my only warmth, it was the purist happiness I've ever felt, until…well, you.

The year that he was five, there was this one toy he really wanted, a stuffed fox that sang the alphabet. They were sold out everywhere. He never got that toy while he was alive.

When he was six and I was twelve, my father beat him so badly that he nearly died. I carried him in my arms, and walked miles until I got to a hospital. The police were called. My father was taken to jail. We were taken to a children's home. It was horrible there, so we ran away and went back home to my mother.

Biggest mistake I ever made. It cost him his life. No, don't argue with me.

My mother was furious with us. She had a sick love-hate relationship with my father. He had stabbed her, fractured her skull, knocked her teeth out, punched her until she miscarried again and again. She slashed him with a broken liquor bottle, and broke his nose with a chair leg while he was passed out drunk. He used to flaunt other women right in front of her, take them home and fuck them in their bed while she was locked out of the room, screaming and beating on the door. She would hunt the women down, cut up their faces or beat their skulls in with bricks.

She was so enraged that my father was in jail because of us, she got rid of us for good. And she made a profit doing it.

She sold us to a couple of men who wanted pretty little boys.

Pyotr was terrified. When we got in that truck I lied and told him that we were going to a nice new home.

That was the last day I ever saw him smile.

Jasha, Maks, Feodyr, Slavik, and a boy named Yakim – I met them all there. Your father and Vilyat came to inspect and approve the new merchandise. They don't remember me, but I still remember them. Oh, believe me, I do. Every contour of their faces. The sound of their voices. Their laughter.

We heard them speak. They gave away quite a lot of information about themselves, because adults always underestimate children, and because none of us were meant to make it out of there alive.

We learned that they were from America, and that they visited Russia every couple of months. We learned that they didn't personally sample the boys, because they preferred girls. We learned their last name. Toporov. It was burned into my memory.

After we were inspected, a few children were disposed of because they had venereal diseases. Your father did that. Took them out the back and shot them in the head, one by one, and we had to watch.

Then we were separated by age. The men who visited that whorehouse had particular tastes. They would want children of a specific age range.

They dragged Pyotr away from me. I fought, but they just laughed at me and beat me until I passed out.

We were there for a couple of months in total. It doesn't sound that long, does it? You can't imagine how long a couple of months can feel.

Yes, we were raped. Every day. Many times a day. We were beaten. Tortured. Starved. If we wanted to eat, we'd have to crawl across the floor and bend over for men to violate us. We were made to submit to unspeakable acts by adult men who laughed at our pain.

They brought in new boys on a regular basis, to replace the boys who died.

We'd been planning our escape since the day we arrived. We stole dull bread knives and sharpened them. We broke the furniture and made weapons from the sharp splinters.

The men had made a mistake, using street rats for their little boy whores. They thought they were being smart. They knew that nobody would miss us. And they liked our spirit; they enjoyed it more when we fought back. But they didn't anticipate how wily, and sneaky, and vicious we already were.

Finally I got word from one of the other boys that Pyotr was sick. He'd developed an infection. We had to act right away if we were to have any chance of saving him.

Our plan was basically a suicide pact. We were as good as dead there anyway; we had nothing to lose. There wasn't a single boy who'd been there longer than six months. Most had only been there three or four. The boys would die of sepsis, or the men would kill them for sport.

We planned to stage an uprising and kill as many men as we possibly could, and we'd get as many boys out as we could. We were deep in the country, but we thought we might just have a chance that some of the boys could escape and go to a news station and tell them what happened. We didn't have any hope of going to the police; the local chief came to visit himself sometimes.

But we were more successful then we'd ever expected.

We actually killed all of the guards and clients. They weren't expecting it, from children. We killed the first few guards, took their guns, and turned the guns on the rest.

Feodyr jumped in front of me and took a bullet for me. It's a miracle he didn't die.

We all ran for it. Pyotr had gone ahead. He was alone in the woods, in the winter.

He was killed by a starving wolf. The wolf was still feeding on him when I found him.

My bracelet? Made from the wolf's sinews. I strangled that wolf with my bare hands.

You know, that toy fox – Jasha, get the fuck away from me – I give Pyotr that fox every single year. I buy him a nice new one and take it to his grave, or have it delivered since I've left the country.

Get her out. Get her out. *Get her out!*"

* * *

WILLOW

Jasha and his men rushed me out of there, and slammed and locked the door behind him. I heard Sergei roaring like a wounded beast.

I'd done that to him.

My family had done that to him.

"He'll hurt himself," I gasp.

"That's why the room is padded." There's not a glint of softness or sympathy in his voice.

I stumble and fall.

Jasha carries me back to my room. Slavik clumps heavily along beside him. They seem dispirited, the life sucked out of them. They've just had the nightmare story of their past recounted, their humiliation and agony dredged up and displayed before a stranger. And their leader, the man whose strength has kept them going, is in the grip of madness.

Jasha sets me down on the bed and backs away. His expression is bleak, and he looks lost.

Slavik's fists clench, and when he speaks to me, disgust ices his every word. "Now you know why we hate you."

Jasha heaved a sigh. "She didn't know. She was not part of it. She is no more guilty of what happened to us than we were."

Slavik spits a stream of curses, then storms out of the room.

I lie on my bed, on my side. I couldn't move if I were drowning.

There is no reason for me to move, to eat, to drink. To breathe.

EIGHTEEN

Who knows what day?

Who cares? I will never have the strength to leave here. I'll die here. I deserve it.

I stagger around my room. I trip over things. I bump into the wall because I can barely see. That's okay. It doesn't hurt. I cannot feel my own body.

The cold white sun tells me it's daylight outside, but what day? What part of the day? Morning, afternoon?

My father's putrid blood taints me.

He used to fly to Russia every couple of months, and when he came back, he'd bring presents for me. Russian nesting dolls. Chocolate eggs with toys in them. Necklaces with charms dangling on them. Beautiful handmade dresses.

I would dance with joy. I would thank him in perfect Russian. My father would nod his approval, which would make my mother smile in relief. She'd trained me well in how to keep him happy.

And the money that financed those trinkets… I ate chocolate and wore beautiful dresses that were purchased with the blood of *child whores*.

And my poor mother. Forced to marry him at such a young age, dragged to this country, away from everything she'd ever known, and she never said a word. To protect me. She was little more than a child, only a few years older than Helenka is now, when she was snatched up by my father.

I knew that my father was a strict, old-fashioned man, and that my mother walked on egg-shells around him, but she hid the true horror of our lives inside her for all those years.

Somewhere, in the back of my mind, I had rationalized our family's dirty dealings. I told myself, nobody forces people to do drugs, do they? And the guns that the criminals used were only used on each other, right?

So I tried to pretend to myself that even though what they were doing was horrible, it was mostly a victimless crime.

Wasn't it?

But this...no.

This stole everything from me. My identity, my past, my mother...all polluted by the bastard who'd fathered me. The man who supplied half of my DNA. Half my flesh is evil. Which half? Could I cut the evil out of me?

I pick up a framed picture from a book shelf, and raise my hand to smash it. I imagine the glass sliding through my flesh, digging out the rotten parts.

Maks snatches it from my hand and slaps my head so hard my ears ring.

I gape at him.

"How long have you been here?"

"Long enough."

"How...how long have I been here?"

"Two days."

Two days?

I remember somebody trying to feed me. I remember gagging.

He looks at me in disgust. "And if you're looking for pity, you're looking in the wrong place."

"I don't deserve pity," I whisper.

"Fucking right. If it were up to me, I'd let you kill yourself."

I walk into the bathroom and collapse to my knees, and dry heave into the toilet. He follows me and stands in the doorway.

I shakily stand up and walk back out. "Is Sergei all right now?" My voice is a rasping husk.

Maks' lip curls as if he'd smelled foul rotting flesh. "If he wants you to know how he's doing, he will tell you himself."

"Yes," I whisper, and stagger back to bed.

A nurse comes in. It's dark outside now. She hands me a glass of water and I drink a little and set it down. My throat is raw. Have I been screaming again? My head pounds dully, but if someone gave me aspirin, I'd spit it out.

"You need to eat," she tells me sternly.

I curl up in a ball and wrap my arms around my head. "Fuck you. Fuck everybody."

Some time later, an hour or a day, Sergei comes in.

He has a fading black eye. His nose is swollen. His lip is cut. He carries a tray with a bowl of stew on it, and sets it down on the side table next to my chair.

"Eat, or I'll shove it down your throat."

I close my eyes. "Okay."

"This self-pity shit isn't doing it for me."

"I know."

A spoon bangs against my mouth.

I taste blood.

He grabs me by the hair and pulls me into a sitting up position.

He holds out the spoon again. Obediently, I let him spoon feed me. I couldn't stop him. All the strength has left my muscles.

"How many days?" I whisper.

"It's the seventeenth day of our agreement."

* * *

Day eighteen...

He feeds me breakfast the next morning. Eggs. Bacon.

He feeds me lunch and dinner again. Bite by bite. He cuts it up into small pieces and slides it into my mouth. I chew without tasting, and swallow.

He barely speaks to me. His eyes are haunted, and I know that's my fault. I dragged up his filthy putrid past and made him relive it. I made him walk over the burning coals of hell again, just to satisfy my curiosity.

* * *

Day nineteen...

He comes in again, setting a tray of food down on the table next to the armchair. I am still in bed. The distance from the bed to the chair felt too far this morning.

I look up at him wearily. The air is leaden and so heavy I can't stand, but he shouldn't have to come in and baby me just because I'm too depressed to move. "I'm sorry I'm like this," I say dully. "I'm sorry about everything."

He's unimpressed. "Sorry doesn't mean shit. Pull yourself together." He glares at me. "What will help you?" he demands. "Do you want to see a therapist?"

"It wouldn't help." It wouldn't miraculously rewrite my past or cleanse my DNA of evil.

At that, he grimaces. "Yep. Tried it a few times. Didn't help me."

"You don't have to try to fix things, Sergei. It's all right."

He gives me a stony look. "I told you I needed you. You're pulling me down with you."

That brings tears to my eyes, but I don't even have the energy to cry.

"I'm sorry," I whisper. "I would do anything to help you. I just can't. I'm not doing this on purpose. There's nothing left of me."

He sighs, and bends down and scoops me up from the bed and carries me to the chair.

He plops down in the chair next to mine and holds up the spoon. "Feed yourself."

I take the spoon and obey, mechanically. I eat fifteen bites, counting each one carefully, then set the spoon down.

He stares off into space for a while before speaking, and his voice is soaked in regret and sorrow. "When I first brought you here...I mistreated you. I shouldn't have. I apologize. All right? It was wrong of me."

"Was it?" Right now I feel as if he wasn't cruel enough to me. He should have burned my flesh. Cut me. Disfigured me. Made my outside as ugly as my insides, as hideous as the DNA that pollutes me.

"Yes. You know it was, Willow." There's an impatient snap to his tone now. "Don't be the fucking martyr. You said it yourself; my fight was with your uncle, not you. When I let your family twist me into a sadist, I let them gain a victory over me that they didn't deserve."

"How can you even touch me?" Tears spill down my cheeks. I am surprised; I didn't think I had any more tears left. I'm not sobbing;

my tears are just flowing as if someone turned on a tap.

"Cut out this self-pity crap, Willow!" He stands up, glowering. "Quit being a spoiled little bitch." I look up at him in shock. I didn't think anything could hurt me any more, but his words are razor-sharp arrows that find their mark.

"Were you kidnapped as a child, held down and raped up the ass by perverted old men every day for months? Were you forced to suck cock after starving for days on end, just to earn a dry slice of bread? Did you find your brother's body being eaten by an animal? No? Then get off the fucking self-pity train."

Every word is a hammer-blow to my chest. I feel myself sinking lower and lower, drowning in a sea of revulsion and self-loathing. Blackness swims in front of me, and I can't see or feel.

"I'm not..." I drag the words up from the slimy depths of my soul. I don't know which direction to look, because there's a wall of darkness in front of my eyes. If I cared about what happened to me, I'd be very frightened by that. "I'm not asking you for pity. I'm not asking you for anything. I don't deserve anything. I'm disgusting. I'm gone. I'm not here. I'm nothing." I keep babbling, spewing words of despair like sewage running from my mouth.

My vision clears, and I see that Sergei is gone.

That is what I deserve.

* * *

Day twenty...

Morning, I think.

Sergei bangs open the door and storms in. I am curled up in my chair again, wearing the same pajamas I've been wearing for days. I can smell my own body odor; I stink like a rotting corpse. I can't believe Sergei can stand to occupy the same airspace.

"Lukas will be here in two minutes. So clean yourself up."

I sit up, shaking all over. "He ca-ca-can't see me like this!" I protest weakly.

"Exactly."

"Two minutes? You couldn't have given me a little more time?"

Sergei snorts. "The world doesn't adapt to your schedule, princess."

I stumble to the bathroom and wash my face. I hear Lukas' voice, calling for me, tugging at my heartstrings. "Willow? My friend Willow?"

Damn it. Why is Sergei doing this to him? Hasn't the poor kid been through enough?

"I'll be right out!" I call. I'm trying for a light, happy voice, but instead I sound shrill and hysterical. I grab my toothbrush and scrub the foul taste from my mouth, and rub deodorant on my reeking pits. I comb my fingers through my tangled hair, and it makes it worse. I look like a witch who stuck her finger in a light socket.

I walk out of the bathroom. Lukas is standing there holding a pad of paper and a tin of colored pencils. He takes one look at me and bursts into tears.

Sergei fixes me with a cold look. "And that's on *you*," he snaps at me. Throwing my own words back at me.

"Where are Kris and Marya?" I demand, looking around frantically. I'm in no shape to take care of a little boy.

"I sent them away until you can get your act together. I don't care if it takes hours or weeks. Right now, you're all he's got." He leans in and whispers harshly. "He used to see his mother like this all the time, right before she overdosed."

She ODed? Who was she? How did Sergei know her?

And just like that, the bastard walks out of the room and slams the door shut behind him, leaving the traumatized little boy with the shell that used to be a woman.

I make my mouth move into the shape of a smile. Apparently it isn't very convincing, because he starts crying, really hard.

I know I can't do this, but I have to at least try.

"I've been sick, Lukas, I'm sorry. I...I have a cold."

"Cold?" He picks up a decorative throw that's draped across my bed and holds it out to me. The sweetest boy on the planet.

"Let's go outside and draw," I say to him.

I grab my pastels and pad of paper, and he takes his paper and pencils, and we go into the garden.

He draws a crying seagull. He draws a crying rose.

I get the picture.

I draw a mother seagull hugging a baby seagull and he smiles a little bit.

We walk around the garden. I spot a particularly lovely rose, a fat pink cabbage-head bobbing on a slender stalk. We sit down on a bench, and he starts sketching, and the rose materializes on the paper, with little beads of dew on it.

Yet again, I marvel at his talent. When he grows up, he could show his pictures in galleries. I praise him, and he lights up like a little tiny sun, warming me with the joy that beams out from him.

The suffocating fog that's been clinging to me seems to have faded. My world hasn't blazed back to technicolor life, but I can at least see colors again.

I realize that Sergei knew exactly how to drag me back to reality. I may be long past giving a damn what happens to me, but I can't make everyone else around me suffer.

I have to stop stewing in a swamp of self-pity. There are people here who care about me, and I'm useless to them if I'm curled up in a stinking ball of B.O. and misery. I have been forever changed, but I will move my numb body again, I will walk and talk and eat like a real girl, and stop being a burden on everyone around me.

For a man who claims to have no soul and no empathy, Sergei is amazingly in tune what those around him need.

As Lukas finishes his picture, it occurs to me how remarkable it is that, once Sergei realized that Lukas loved to draw, he made sure that he had art supplies. Vilyat would literally have broken Yuri's fingers if he'd seen him sketching. He would have raged that no son of his was a pussy little faggot homo artist.

Sergei is the most macho, masculine, badass man that I'd ever met. He is built from tank parts and fueled with testosterone, but he is completely comfortable with encouraging Lukas to nourish his artistic talent.

He's a better man than he lets himself admit. He's a better man than any of the men in my family, any of the men I grew up with. He is tormented and torn apart by his inner demons, but if there weren't some good left in him, he wouldn't be so conflicted by his own actions.

It speaks to his core decency that despite all the brutal blows that life has dealt him, he still cares for others. I think that underneath it all, he's more like his little brother Pyotr than he lets himself admit. And I understand why he tries to shove that soft side of him deep, deep into the darkness. Pyotr was soft and sweet, after all, and look what happened to him.

Lukas and I head inside the house and a maid takes us to the drawing room, and Sergei is waiting for us. He's sitting there reading a book on military strategy, in Russian, and he nods at me but doesn't say anything. Lukas sings me songs in Czech until Kris and Marya come to get him. I hug him goodbye and kiss the top of his head.

"Thanks," I say to Sergei, after they're gone. "I'm sorry."

"Stop saying that. Seriously. It pisses me off." He puts the book down and gets up to leave. Then he turns back, his gaze catching and holding mine. "I will see you in your room tonight after dinner."

NINETEEN

Day twenty...

I've showered, washed and de-tangled my hair, and I look human again. The view out of my garden window frames a night scene with a slice of crescent moon hovering in a star-spangled sky. I'm sitting in front of my easel sketching a still life of a vase and cut roses, when I hear Sergei's footsteps in the hall.

The warm arousal that seeps through me whispers that my flesh has come back to life.

I feel his presence even before he enters. He strolls through the door, stopping by the side of my chair. He reaches down and trails his fingers along my jaw with a feather-light touch and then in the gentlest voice he's ever used, says, "Take off your clothing for me, Willow. Then lie down on the bed, on your back. I just want to look at you."

Normally when he speaks softly, there's enormous pain following immediately afterwards, but somehow, tonight, I sense he won't hurt me.

30 DAYS OF SHAME

As if in a dream, I pull my shirt over my head. I unhook my bra. I slide off my pants and panties together in one smooth motion and drop them on the floor.

While I'm doing this, Sergei's eyes never leave me. His hands glide over his shirt, undoing buttons, then down to his zipper, then slide his pants down, but all his focus is on my body. His gaze sweeps me like a warm caress, and I feel my flesh heating and growing more sensitive.

I look at him through-half lidded eyes. I've never really studied his body before. When he took me before, he was mostly dressed, and I was usually dazed with fear and lust. Focused on surviving the pain that he dished out to me, and worse, the agonizing way he teased my body and made me crave him.

Now I'm noticing not just the broad chest and that tapers to the V of his torso, but the patchwork of war wounds on his skin. Bullet holes. Knife slashes. Puckered splatters of burned skin.

He looms over me, and my nipples swell, rising towards him. Then he slides onto the bed, on top of me, and he kisses my mouth with a soft tenderness. He bites my lower lip ever so gently, and I whimper in pleasure.

His long, slow kisses are thorough and searching and gentle, his tongue sliding against mine in an exquisitely erotic caress that has me moaning softly against his mouth. He runs his hands over my body, stroking and teasing, setting up quivers of sensation in my flesh wherever he touches me.

Warily at first, but then with growing confidence, I let my hands explore his body. Big, rugged, the raised flesh of those cruel scars textured beneath my touch. I explore them with my fingers, tracing their edges with feather-light touches. He's never let me touch him like this before. I know he thinks it makes him weak, vulnerable. But tonight he tolerates it. Wants it, from the way his breath quickens.

He draws back for a moment, breaking the kiss, and I feel bereft, but he holds himself above me with one strong arm, muscles bulging and straining, and with his free hand he fits the head of his cock against my drenched pussy. He's huge and hard, and I want him inside me so badly it's a fierce ache.

He groans as he pushes himself inside me, and it's a haunting sound – raw and vulnerable – and I wrap my arms around him and hold him close as he starts to move inside me, pushing his hips against mine to get as deeply inside me as he can, swearing softly against my neck in Russian.

He thrusts inside me again and again, his cock dragging over my G-spot every time he withdraws, and tension coils between my thighs. I gasp and arch my hips to meet him, shuddering with pleasure. I clutch the muscular globes of his ass, urging him inside me harder and faster, but he continues to fuck me slowly, thoroughly. I reach up to trace the silvery scar that slashes through his eyebrow with my thumb. His eyes are closed, the harsh lines of his face set in an expression of raw, open need that makes me want to weep.

Long, sweet shudders of bliss are running through my body now, and my breathing turns into a series of harsh little gasps as orgasm blooms and unfurls inside me. He gives a strangled groan and his cock kicks inside me, then he muffles his shouts of release against my skin as my pussy spasms around him and we cling to each other, riding out the shocks of bliss that rock through us, leaving us limp and senseless.

He lies down behind me and wraps his arms around me. We're slick with sweat. Gradually our breathing slows. I can feel every beat of his heart thrumming against my back, and I start to relax more and more. Gradually, sleep rolls in, and for the first night in weeks I don't toss and turn for hours.

But when I wake up, I instantly sense his absence.

"Sergei?" I call out to him. "Where are you?"

He's gone. He's left me again.

* * *

Day twenty-one...

A maid taps on the door in the morning, and tells me that breakfast will be ready in twenty minutes. As I climb into the shower, I allow myself to hope.

And to my amazement, he's actually there, waiting for me in the dining room. The table is spread with the usual amazing feast – mountains of bacon and piles of fluffy eggs and stacks of pancakes dripping with sweetly scented maple syrup. I manage a tiny smile as I sit down and spoon lumps of sugar into my coffee.

I understand now why Sergei's meals are always an exercise in excess, why after a childhood of starvation, he must pile up the richest, most delicious food at every meal. And I ache at the thought of child-Sergei's growling stomach.

"You're feeling better?" Sergei asks, and shoves a forkful of potatoes into his mouth.

I sip my coffee and consider the question before answering. "I don't feel like I did before, and I don't think I ever will again. It's hard to put into words, but...my entire body feels different, because I'm built from different materials then I was led to believe. It's like I was told I was fashioned from gold, but it was really lead. Everything that I thought was true about myself is a lie. I feel different from the inside out. I'll start to forget, I'll start to feel a little better, and then it comes rushing back to me and I feel disgusting all over again."

"Yes. That happens after a trauma," Sergei says solemnly. "But you just keep moving forward and doing what needs to be done every day. And it fades, bit by bit. It never goes away, though."

I can't let myself think about the kind of traumas that Sergei has endured, and how it must have felt for him to move through endless days and nights.

But I can actually smell the food today, and I'm having breakfast with Sergei, and even if everything is a little duller and uglier, it's not hideous and painful at the moment.

So I ladle eggs onto my plate and stack up some pancakes. And the food tastes as good as it looks.

Sergei is silent as he eats, but that's all right. His presence here, with me, speaks volumes. Usually after we're intimate, he avoids me for days, but we lay together hours ago in the tenderest encounter we've ever had, and here he is with me again.

As we sit there, Maks walks up to us, holding my phone, the one that was taken from me when I first arrived at Sergei's house. There's a sour look pinching his face. "Anastasia. Wants to speak to Willow." He spits the words out like lumps of rotten meat. I reach for the phone, but he hands it to Sergei instead.

"Listen, you spoiled little bitch," Sergei barks into the phone. "If you say one more word to upset Willow, I will hunt you down, and Vilyat's worst tortures will seem like sweet, sweet mercy."

"Sergei!" I cry. "Don't talk to her like that!"

He slaps the phone into my palm, his eyes dark as a stormy sea.

"Anastasia," I say. "I didn't expect to hear from you again."

"I just want to say that I am sorry about what I told you," she says, sounding lost and sad. "I shouldn't have dragged you down with me."

"No, you did the right thing telling me. I needed to know."

"Maybe. But I didn't tell you from unselfish motivations. I was angry, I was frustrated. And I was on the defensive. I'm not saying that you're wrong about wanting me to go to the police. I'm just saying that I have to do what is right for my children. They will never grow up knowing the kind of life I led." There's an edge of sharp steel to her voice when she says that.

"I understand." I rub my face with my hands. I'm doing that a lot these days. My flesh feels dirty, and no matter how hard and long I scrub in the shower, an invisible grit clings to me. "And I shouldn't have said that you were dead to me. When I get angry, I lash out. You're my family. You always will be." I sigh. "But I won't give up on this, Anastasia."

"Things will change soon, I'm sure." She's speaking cryptically, but I am sure she means that Vilyat will die soon enough.

So I reply cryptically. "The change will be too small."

Logically I know that people are being trafficked all over the world, and it will never stop. But the knowledge that she has information that could save women from torture right now, and she's choosing not to – it's a bitter pill to swallow.

"How is Lukas?" She's not even subtle about changing the subject.

"Fine. I'm sure he misses Helenka and Yuri. How are they?"

"So far everything is all right. Helenka's being kind of quiet and serious. Not her usual jokey self. We're staying at a condo complex with very good security. We're on the first floor, so we never have to get in an elevator or take the stairs. Vilyat signed all the papers I wanted him to sign, and he gave me two million dollars, and he paid my lawyers, and I haven't heard a word from him. You could come stay with us," she added hopefully.

"Not until certain things happen." Like her going to the cops with what she has on Vilyat.

"I see." That's all she says. Then she clears her throat.

"Is Jasha okay? Could you tell him I say hi, and the kids miss his lessons?"

"No, I will not. You want to tell him, come and do it yourself. I should go. I love you, Anastasia, but I'm really disappointed in you as well, on a level I can't even communicate. You are allowing bad things to happen. You could help people, and you choose not to."

"I love you too. You took care of my children for so long. And me, you took care of me. After I gave up on life. You pulled me back out of the shadows. You told me I was worth saving, and finally I believed you. Take care of yourself, Willow, I hope I can see you soon."

When I hang up, I look around for Maks, but he's gone. I try to hand the phone back to Sergei. He shakes his head.

"Keep it," he says. He takes an enormous swig of his coffee.

I look at him in surprise. "Really? So you're not worried that I'll try to call for help?"

"Call who?" he asks. "And not to be a dick, but where would you even go? You're broke and homeless and completely dependent on me. Unless you want to trade your morals for security, and move in with your aunt after all."

I scowl at him. "Wow, no, that wasn't dickish at all." I set the phone down next to my plate, feeling glum and deflated.

He's right. And there are seven days left until my thirty days are up. Will he really kick me out? Or give me the house and leave? Or let me stay with him?

I don't dare ask, so I just jab at my pancakes with my fork and watch them bleed syrup, and imagine it's Vilyat's red, red blood.

TWENTY

Day twenty-two...

Last night he came to me and woke me from sleep, and we had sex again, and he was a little rougher this time. He held my hands over my head, and cupped my chin in his hand and made me look at him when I came. He lay with me for hours afterwards, stroking me softly. But he still wouldn't sleep in the same bed with me.

He skipped breakfast, but at eleven a.m. he comes to find me when I'm out for a stroll in the garden. He's wearing a light gray linen suit and he smells like spicy cologne and testosterone.

"We're going out to lunch. Don't fucking argue with me," Sergei growls as I open my mouth to protest that I'm not up for it.

I drop my gaze. "I wasn't going to argue."

"Yes, actually, you were. I know the look on your face, the way your body moves, when you're about to argue with me. So you're lying to me. Are you that hard up for a spanking?" His eyes gleam.

I snort. "Sergei, you say the sweetest things."

That earns me a dirty look. "If I start acting sweet, someone has put a microchip in my brain and is controlling my thoughts. Please have me shot and put out of everyone's misery."

"The thought's entered my head. More than once," I say wryly.

"Oh really? Have I reminded you lately who's in charge, little Willow?" He grabs my butt cheek and squeezes hard. I jerk, and gasp in pain and arousal. I loved it when he was sweet and tender a couple of days ago, but this is my drug. It's crack cocaine, it's a mountain-size chocolate fudge sundae, it's an endorphin rush that I'd die for. I realize how much I've missed when he torments me.

"We could go a little later," I say to him.

"I know that's what you want. That's why I'm going to make you wait. It's part of your punishment."

I stare at him, wonderingly. "You are an evil son of a bitch."

At that, he winks, with a grim smile. "Now who's saying sweet things? Be dressed in fifteen minutes, or I'll shove something up your ass that makes you cry like a baby."

Damn it. When he says things like that I want to tear off my clothes and lick him from head to toe.

I go to my room, smiling and feeling warm all over. I walk into my closet and a sudden panic attack swamps me like a tidal wave and I sink to my knees, gasping. I'm ice cold. I'm shaking.

Ugly voices scream at me.

You're joking around while women are being raped? You're flirting while they're being tortured? Being murdered? Selfish bitch, selfish bitch, selfish bitch...

Your father sold little children! You deserve nothing but pain! Selfish bitch, selfish bitch, selfish bitch...

I clench my fists and my nails sink into my palms. *I should hit myself. I should bang my head on the wall until I crack my skull open and let my brains leak out.*

"Willow?" Sergei is standing above me.

"Oh!" I gasp, and start violently. The voices fade and vanish. I gape up at him. "I lost an earring."

He reaches down and grabs my hand, and pulls me to my feet.

"There it is. In your ear. It matches the other one you're wearing."

"I am?" My hand flutters to my ears.

"What you meant to say was that you were having a panic attack. Here, wear this." He shoves a white silk A-line dress at me, and stands there and waits.

I strip out of my slacks and T-shirt and change, feeling incredibly grateful that he isn't trying to talk to me about my feelings or chastise me for my weakness. He's just there, giving me exactly what I need, no more, no less.

How does he know how to give me exactly what I need?

When I trudge out to the car, I can't say the panic attack is completely gone. The screaming voices frightened and disoriented me, and my heart is still beating faster and I'm breathing too quickly, but I remind myself that I don't have to feel okay all the time. I just have to keep moving forward. One foot in front of the other.

Sometimes I will be okay. Sometimes I will feel horrible. Whether I am feeling good or bad, the most important thing to remember is: *this too shall pass.*

The restaurant is half an hour away, in a small, charming downtown seaside village. Sergei orders the wine for us, and I choose a seafood salad. His bodyguards are with us, of course, and they sit at a table right next to us.

When I get up to go to the bathroom, I feel oddly light, like a balloon whose string has been slashed. I realize that this is the first time I've gone out with Sergei, without someone following at my heels. It's a real date. Not a hostage situation. That thought wrenches a shaky laugh from me.

As I stand at the sink washing my hands, my phone rings. It's Anastasia's ring tone.

When I answer, she's shrill with panic.

"He's got her!"

My heart leaps into my throat. I don't have to ask who has who. "When?" I demand.

"I don't know, I was on my computer when Yuri came in and gave me a note she'd left on her bed. The note said she'd run away because I won't tell her what's going on with her father. She could have been gone for as long as a couple of hours by then. Then right after that, like two minutes ago, I got a call from her phone. It was Vilyat." Her voice rises higher and higher, she's almost screaming into the phone. "He grabbed her up when she was in the parking lot outside the condo. He says that I must call up the news stations right away and tell them that I was lying about him beating me, and I must give him full custody of both kids, and transfer back all the money, and check myself into a mental institution, or I will never see her again. What do I do? If I just give him all the money would he give her back?"

Stay calm, stay calm… "Let me ask Sergei. Don't do anything until I call you back. Don't fall for his threats. Even if you do everything he asks, he won't ever let you have the kids again."

She sobs. "Oh, God, please save her, Willow. I'll turn the information over to the police. I'll do anything."

"I will call you right back. Sergei will save her. I know he will." I don't know that, but I cannot accept any other outcome.

Before I can leave the room, my phone rings again. It's Helenka's phone, but I know that it won't be her calling.

I answer it, my insides liquid with terror.

"Listen to me, you little slut," Vilyat snarls. I hear Helenka sobbing in the background. Helenka never cries. What has he done to her?

The rage that burns through me is the purest, truest thing I've ever felt. *I will fucking end him.*

"You are in the bathroom of the Salty Dog. Go climb out the window and run across the parking lot. You will see a blue van there waiting for you."

So he had someone follow Sergei's car here. "Fine. I will trade myself for Helenka. If you want me, you have to let her go."

"You don't get to bargain with me, you traitorous bitch!" Vilyat roars. I hear a smacking sound, and Helenka screams. It takes everything I have not to cry out in fury.

"You want leverage against Sergei," I say, keeping my voice steady. I am about to die, or be raped or tortured. I know this. But Helenka's life depends on me keeping calm. "He doesn't care less about her. He cares about me. You will let her go, and I will go with you and do anything that you say."

I hang up before he can answer.

I climb out of the window, and fall awkwardly to the ground. I pull my little canister of mace out of my purse, and flip the top up, and run halfway across the parking lot. The cursedly empty parking lot. Nobody to help me, nobody to hear me scream. God, I wish I still had my taser, or better, a gun.

I see the van, engine running, waiting.

The door slides open. I see Helenka and Vilyat, and a man pointing a gun at Helenka's head. Her face is contorted with terror. I want to fall to the ground and die, but I stand up straight, for her.

"Let her out," I call. "I'm not getting in until she's free."

The door closes and the van starts to slowly move away.

I force myself to stand there. It's the hardest thing I've ever done, but I have no choice.

Finally the car backs up and the door opens. Helenka and the man climb out. He has her arm twisted up behind her back, and her mouth is open in a wordless wail.

"Let go of her," I call. I walk closer. She's so pale, she looks so wretched and helpless…they've beaten Warrior Helenka into a terrified child. I can see red marks all over her face, where she's been hit, and her lip is bleeding.

I am almost on top of them, but I stay out of his reach.

I hear a group of people talking now, around the corner, by the side of the restaurant. He hears it too; his eyes dart nervously in the direction of their voices.

The man lets go of her, and rushes forward, and grabs me by the arm. She starts to stumble away, and he grabs her again, and now he's dragging both of us towards the van. I fumble with my mace and he jerks me violently, making me drop it and fall to my knees.

The expression on Helenka's face changes in a flash.

As smooth as can be, she kicks him in the crotch so hard he doubles over, letting go of both of us. She kicks him again, in the jaw, so hard I hear it crunch. Blood pours out of his mouth. It was all an act! A beautiful, beautiful act. Thank God for Jasha. Without his teaching, she'd be back in the van already.

Another man shoots out of the car and grabs me as I'm staggering back to my feet, and I scream at Helenka. "Sergei is in the restaurant, go to him, run, run!"

Helenka flies across the parking lot with her feet barely touching the ground, around the corner, shrieking at the top of her lungs the whole way. Her shrill child's voice sings in the wind. "Kidnappers! Perverts! They're kidnappers, they tried to kidnap me, they tried to rape me, kidnappers, rape, rape, rape!" Instantly I hear answering shouts, getting closer.

It's too late, though. I'm hauled into the van, clawing and biting and thrashing. The van door slams. I know I won't win, but I vow to go down fighting.

Vilyat is behind the wheel. The van screeches out of the parking lot.

I am on the floor, flailing and kicking. A man slaps me across the face so hard my head bounces off the door. Then a reeking cloth is forced over my mouth and nose. *Chloroform.* I try to hold my breath, but someone punches me in the stomach, forcing me to suck in air, and everything goes dark.

TWENTY-ONE

Day twenty-one?

It's the smell that wakes me up. My eyes are shut, my world is dark, but the smell of urine and blood forces its way into my nostrils.

I gag and suck in air through my mouth, but the stench is so strong I can taste it. Bit by bit, unwelcome consciousness sweeps the fog from my head.

I don't dare open my eyes, for fear of what I'll see, but I know I've been stripped naked. My hands and feet are chained to a mattress. Terror chews at me.

Sergei will never find me.

It's the end.

At least Helenka got away. I pray that Sergei will offer Helenka and Yuri and my aunt protection until he can find Vilyat and kill him. He has to know that would be my final wish. My dying wish.

Footsteps thud towards my bed, and I tense, bracing myself for whatever's coming next. An ice-cold explosion of water smashes into me, and I yank violently against my chains and open my eyes, gasping. My vision swims into focus and I stare up at a man looming over me. I don't recognize him; he's got a squarish, acne-scarred face and a nose that skews off to the left. He's holding an empty bucket, which he drops on the floor with a clatter.

"You look like a drowned rat," he sneers.

My mouth is dry, or I'd spit on him. "You look like a dead man walking," I rasp. "Sergei's going to make you into dog food."

"Is that right? Well, I should have some fun with his girl first, then." He smirks and runs his hand down my stomach. I go rigid with revulsion. My skin wants to crawl away from him. He squats down until his hot, foul breath is fanning my face, and shoves his finger up inside me. I stay stiff, refusing to move or struggle. I pretend it's a tampon. I freeze my face into stone. I look at his face without seeing it, imagining the ocean, building a picture to block out his image.

He looks disappointed at my lack of reaction, and slides his finger back out. "You're a pig-ugly bitch, but I'm gonna fuck you anyway. Because I know you don't want me to."

I meet his gaze. Sooner or later, I know I will break, but I'm going to make him miserable in every way possible for as long as I can. "Sounds like a personal problem."

He slaps my face. I stifle a cry.

"Mommy didn't hug you when you were growing up?" I taunt him. If I can make him angry enough to kill me, then I'll be spared the rape and torture that's surely coming.

"Shut up, whore!"

"Or maybe she hugged you too much." He slaps me again. "Or was it Daddy?"

He punches me in the side of the head. Sparks explode behind my eyes. "Ooh, I struck a nerve," I gasp.

He cocks his arm back, and I can't help but flinch, because this one's going to hurt.

But a strange feeling swells up inside me, a feeling of power. I'm tied down, naked, and I'm still jerking his strings.

He's weak where it counts. I'm strong where it counts.

Maybe I can manipulate him into untying me. I've got a few tricks that he'd never expect. Yeah, I'll end up dead no matter what, but the thought of getting in some final blows, maybe even killing him, lights a beautiful flame inside me.

Suddenly I'm not weak and disgusting, polluted by my own genetics. I'm a warrior planning a campaign of resistance.

He punches me on the side of the head, and I grunt in pain. Tears flow down my cheeks.

But at the same time, I flex my face into a manic grin.

"What the hell you smiling at, bitch?" he shouts, eyes bulging with rage.

Yes.

I stare right up at him. "My uncle has big plans for me, and they don't include dying at the hands of a yapping Chihuahua like you. So I'm picturing how, after you kill me, he's going to cut you up into little bits while you're still alive, and feed you to sharks."

His face contorts with dismay. It's true, and he knows it – if he kills me, he'll be in deep shit and then he'll die.

He kicks the bed frame in frustration.

Yes.

"I can make you wish I'd killed you," he spits.

"All right then. Let's get this party started, little man."

He kicks the bed again and again, in a frenzy.

Yes, yes, yes. Even though I'm dizzy from the blow to the head, I feel like I'm soaring with triumph.

"Biiiiiitch!" he howls, helpless with thwarted rage. He raises his fist to hit me again.

"Stop hitting her! Stop!" someone wails.

I twist on the bed, looking around the room for the first time. I think we're in a mobile home. The windows are all blacked out and the lights are dim, but not so dim that I fail to see a girl who's chained to a wall maybe ten feet from me. She's also stripped naked, and her hair is limp and stringy. There are bruises all over her abdomen.

My body tenses.

And an evil smile twists the man's mouth.

His creepy gaze skitters from her to me and back again. "You think she's a virgin? I don't think she's no virgin. I'm going to find out."

"No!" I cry out, and instantly regret it. I'm so, so stupid. I've just encouraged him to hurt her, and all she did was beg him not to hit me.

He swaggers over to her, and bends down and bites her left nipple so hard she howls in agony.

Then he goes and fetches a revolver from a cabinet, and walks over to her, and he thrusts the gun up between her legs. He forces the barrel up inside her vagina, violently. She screams and screams, her eyes bulging with terror.

"I just remembered, she ain't a virgin. Cause I popped her cherry for her yesterday. You shoulda been here, she screamed real pretty."

"Please don't," I cry. "Please. I'm sorry. Take me instead. I'll do anything you want."

"Oh, I'm going to take you in every hole you got. Right after I play Russian roulette with this bitch's cunt."

He spins the cylinder on the revolver and then pulls the trigger. She faints in terror.

He slides the gun out, walks over to the bucket, grabs it, and takes it to the sink. She is sagging on her chains. He fills the bucket up, and carries it over and dumps it on her head to wake her up again.

She thrashes and cries. He goes to fetch the revolver from the counter.

I bite my lip to keep from screaming and begging. It's what he wants, so I won't give it to him.

"Do you feel lucky today, bitch?" he croons to the woman hanging from her chains. He slides the gun in again.

"No, no, no, no, no!" she screams.

The door bangs open, and light floods the room. A man sticks his head through and looks at him.

"You fucking idiot," the man snarls. "She's worth fifty grand easy. You going to pay Vilyat fifty grand after you shoot her in the snatch?"

Reluctantly, the man slides the gun out of the woman's vagina. He starts to head back towards me, and a sickening wave of relief that leaves me gasping. Nothing he could do to me is worse than watching him abuse that girl. Then there's a cry from outside.

"We're under attack!" a man shouts.

Our tormentor runs out of the room.

I hear shots, and curses.

Sergei. Please, please, please…

A little while later, Jasha runs in the room, and I start to sob with relief. He has a bolt cutter. He cuts my chains and takes his jacket off, and gives it to me. I put it on. Fortunately, he's huge and I'm short, so it covers me. Then he frees the girl hanging on the wall. She falls to the ground, on her knees, and cries and cries. Jasha sheds his T-shirt and gives it to her, and she pulls it on quickly, hugging herself. Trying to shield herself from touch, from abuse, with those skinny arms of hers.

Jasha pulls me to my feet. I'm still weak and shaky from pain and terror and whatever knockout drug they gave me. There are no more shouts and no more gunshots.

"Helenka!" I cry out. "Oh God, is she all right?"

"She's fine. She's back at Sergei's house with Yuri and her mother. They're very worried about you."

"Where is Sergei?" I demand.

"He's busy. I'm going to take you home." He sees the look of hurt and bewilderment on my face, and he adds, "He's busy with Vilyat."

And that actually makes me smile, despite everything. Because that means that me and Anastasia and my cousins are finally safe.

"All right then," I say.

More men pour into the room. One of them has a blanket, and he wraps it around the girl and picks her up in his arms.

"Let's go. Don't worry about her; she'll be taken to the hospital," Jasha says, and he has to hold me up as I stumble out into the daylight.

I sway on my feet, trying to orient myself. Where the hell am I? I don't recognize this place. It's twilight. We're in a wooded area at the end of a dirt road, and there's another trailer huddled next to the one I was in. There are a dozen cars parked on the grass, scattered around the trailers. There are men lying in the dirt, leaking out their life's blood, empty eyes staring up at the sky.

I catch a glimpse of Sergei hustling a man with a bag over his head into the back of a van.

Vilyat.

Jasha helps me into the back seat of an SUV, and I curl up there, shaking all over. As he drives me back to the house, I remember a joke Sergei made earlier, about a microchip. And I know how Sergei found me.

TWENTY-TWO
SERGEI

Day twenty-one...

"Nice of you to join us," I say to Jasha as he hurries into the back of the warehouse.

He blinks in the blazing fluorescent lights. I've lit this room up like the sun; I don't want to miss a thing. "Oh, good, you didn't start without me," he says, squinting.

"Are you kidding? After all these years? I would never." I grin. "We've all just been enjoying the show while we waited for you."

Vilyat has already pissed and shit himself with terror. I had him stripped naked and tied up, hanging from his hands in this private warehouse that I own, waiting for Jasha.

All my men are there, lined up, watching.

The air crackles with anticipation. We have waited for this moment for so long. We always knew it was possible that one of Vilyat's enemies would get to him first. That was the risk we ran, with our long, drawn-out campaign of terror. But luck smiled on us, and we have him now.

I'm on a manic high. Willow is safe. There were six girls being held in the trailers; they're all being cared for now, recovering, after my men dropped them off in the parking lot of a supermarket minutes from a hospital. Vilyat's henchmen are all dead.

With all the heat on Vilyat right now, it was insane that he kidnapped those girls. College students partying at a night-club, waitresses, a girl stepping outside her apartment for a smoke…they babbled their stories to my men as they were driven to safety. Vilyat had his men roofie them, or grab them as they walked to their cars after work. He just couldn't stop himself.

It's a sickness with him, with all the Toporov men. They get high off torture, and the softer and sweeter their victims, the more exciting it is for them. They make my dark desires seem vanilla and sweet by comparison.

Well, now he's going to get more than a taste of his own medicine.

I walk over to a table full of cruel instruments, and pick up a skinning knife. He sees it, and shrieks and bucks and kicks.

"I'll pay you anything!" he pleads. "I'll work for you for free. I'll let my wife and kids go, forever, I'll never pursue them again. I'll let Willow go."

I just look at him, stroking the blade of my knife like a lover.

"They're already gone," I tell him. "They're my family now. They all hate you, did you know that? Not just your wife. Your children. They feel nothing but contempt and disgust for you. You're a failure as a human being, and a failure as a father."

I walk up to him and he tries to squirm away from me. I draw a thin, shallow line vertically down his stomach, the same way he does to his victims when he's finished with them. Except I only cut the skin.

"Who is *Cataha*?" I demand, on a hunch. *Cataha* guts his victims the same way Vilyat does. Maybe the two of them worked together at some point.

"Satan?" His bloodshot eyes widen in bewilderment. "I'm…I'm a Christian…" he snivels. Riiiight. Yes, he has been known to go to church now and then. And he's a Christian like I'm a fucking Martian.

I punch him in the stomach, and he whimpers in pain. "*Cataha*. The trafficker in Russia." I jab his chest with the tip of the knife.

"I've never heard of him. I can find him for you! Do you want him?" So desperately eager to please me.

My men are crowded around me now. I slash another line across Vilyat's belly, right next to the first one. "No, I've got what I want right here."

"I can make you rich!" he screams, mindless with pain and terror.

"Really?" I say gently. "How? Maybe we could go into business together dealing in little boy whores?"

His eyes light up. He gasps with relief. Idiot.

"Yes! You like little boys? I can get you all the little boys you like, all day long! I've got a house full of them back in Russia; they're all brand new! Most of them haven't even been fucked yet! Sweet, innocent…" Then he sees the look on my face.

And he figures it out, finally.

"*You*…you were from the orphanage. I think I remember now. The way you looked at me. Those eyes…"

"Orphanage?" I punch him in the nose and it breaks with a satisfying crunch. "You mean the child sex-slave whorehouse?"

Vilyat wails in agony. "Oh fuck, oh fuck…I should have killed you then…for looking at me like that…"

"Yes, you should have." I punch him again and break his jaw.

No symphony could ever sound sweeter than the noises Vilyat is making right now.

"Your customers raped my little brother. His name was Pyotr. He's the reason you're going to die before the sun goes down." A wave of wild euphoria floods through me. I've been rehearsing those words in my head for fourteen years. *Fourteen. Fucking. Years.*

Jasha approaches with a bullwhip. His eyes are black as sin and he's shaking with the need for vengeance. "Let me," he begs.

I step back.

"Go," I say. Jasha slashes Vilyat with the whip so hard that blood pours out of him. Vilyat howls to the heavens – just like Jasha did when the men at Vilyat's whorehouse tore into him.

Then Slavik takes a turn.

Then Maks.

The coppery reek of Vilyat's blood coats our nostrils.

My men are sweating and grunting with effort, gasping with satisfaction. It's everything we've dreamed of.

I push forward and shove the knife blade up against Vilyat's crotch. "Tell me where you're keeping the little boys, or I'll cut your dick off," I say.

"No, no, noooo…." For a man who likes to dish out pain, he sure can't take it. I approach him with my knife. I start to saw away at the root of his limp, dangling cock, slowly, and he goes mad, screeching like a woman. Kicking his legs. What does he need his dick for? He's going to be dead soon anyway. He'll never get to use it again.

He vomits on himself.

Then he tells me.

Jasha hurries out of the room to make a phone call to one of our best connections – the Russian journalist, Akim. We work with Akim and the newspaper *Reforma* so much, they're practically business partners. *Reforma* doesn't know that we created Akim, and they're puppets whose strings we jerk. That's okay. They have their job to do, we have ours.

We'll have the children freed within a few hours.

Of course, after what Vilyat and his men put them through, they'll never really be free. I know that better than anyone.

While Jasha is on the phone, I slowly saw away at Vilyat.

I let each of my men have more turns with the bullwhip, with knives, with cattle prods inserted in places that make Vilyat scream and convulse until he passes out. Watching them at work is every bit as satisfying as doing it myself.

We manage to stretch it out for hours. I wish we could make it last longer.

Finally his last tortured breath whispers from his body, and he dangles, limp and lifeless, his toes trailing through a pool of his spilled fluids.

A good man would feel sick at what I just did. As we leave, I feel clean and light and free. I am not a good man.

TWENTY-THREE

SERGEI

Day twenty-four...

It's nine a.m. Willow has a concussion and she gets dizzy when she walks, so she's been taking it easy in bed the last couple of days. I've been busy with our final project, which is unfolding over the next few days, but my craving for her is distracting me again, so I finally give in to it.

If I let myself be with her like a normal man, sleeping with her every night, spending time with her every day, if I didn't force myself to stay away from her for days on end...I wouldn't be consumed with these fits of desire that pull me away from urgent business. But if I did that, I'd grow accustomed to the peace and lightness that only she can grace me with. And I can never do that.

She's sitting up in bed, propped up on a mountain of pillows. The right side of her face is swollen and splotched purple and blue. Helenka, Yuri and Anastasia are sitting with her. Yuri's holding a storybook that he must have been reading to her. I see some drawings on her night-table that are clearly Lukas' work. That kid's got talent, it can't be denied. Of course, Willow was the one to spot it; she sees the best in everybody.

Willow manages a weak smile. The rest of them look at me warily. We've reached a shaky truce. Vilyat's dead, but after months of being on the run and jumping at every shadow, they don't feel safe yet. So they're back at my house for now, but not my prisoners any longer. Of course, they still don't fully trust me. That's smart; their instincts are right on track. I'm not a man who should be trusted.

"You guys run along," Willow says to them. "I'll see you after lunch."

They stand up. "Watch yourself," Helenka says to me. "I've got my eye on you. I know where you sleep."

I do admire her fiery spirit. Even if she is a Toporov. "Fair warning. I sleep very lightly. With a gun under my pillow."

She snorts. "Jasha says it's stupid to brag about things like that. Why tell your enemies what you have prepared for them?"

"If Jasha told you to jump off a bridge, would you do it?"

"Only if I knew I could land directly on you," Helenka says smartly. She and Yuri laugh and high five each other.

They file out of the room, and I settle down next to Willow. She has circles under her eyes and the bruises are really in bloom now, dark against her pale skin.

I trace them very lightly with my fingertips. "How are you feeling?"

"Forget about me. How are *you* feeling? Now that he's gone?"

She looks at me searchingly. There's genuine concern in her eyes. Even lying in her bed like this, in pain, dizzy, she is worried about me rather than herself.

After everything I've done to her.

She should loathe the sight and smell of me.

But she doesn't. She can't. Her heart is so strong, she's still her good self, even after exposure to a toxin like me.

I smile at her gently. "A burden that I have been carrying for years has been lifted from me." I lean in and brush my lips across hers. Her lips part with a soft moan.

Blood rushes to my groin and makes me stiff and achy with need, so I move back. If she weren't injured, I'd take her right here, rough and hard.

"So that's it?" she says to me. "The end of your mission?"

There's a couple more loose ends that will be taken care of shortly, but the less she knows about my business, the safer she is.

"All wrapped up with a nice little bow."

She leans against me, her head resting on my shoulder. Sweet and soft and trusting. "Stay with me? Just for a little while?"

I shouldn't, but with Willow, my behavior has never been rational. Not since the first moment I saw her, badly hidden behind a cluster of potted palms in her uncle's house. Slim, trembling, eyes huge with fright. Something about her called to me on an animal level, and I fell into her web without even realizing it. I stalked her like prey, but who's the prisoner now?

Ever since that day, I've been lying to myself. I lied to myself when I demanded that her uncle give me one of his children as collateral. I always knew it would be Willow who'd submit her tender flesh to me as a sacrifice. I lied to myself when I told myself that I'd destroy her just for fun, as collateral damage in my war against the Toporov men. I lied to myself when I pretended to believe that it would be easy to walk away from her when I was finished with my campaign of revenge.

And now look where my lies have gotten me.

Hopelessly obsessed with the kindest, strongest women I've ever met, and with no hope of a future for us. It's a horrible fate that I richly deserve.

Always a glutton for punishment, I peel back the covers and slide into bed next to her, pulling her slim body up against mine. I wrap my arms around her and breathe in her honeyed scent. Her small, round butt is pressed up against my crotch, and my erection throbs in response.

"How did you find me at Vilyat's trailer?" she murmurs. "You didn't follow us there. So how?"

I dodge the question. "I'm good at what I do." I stroke her slender arm, trailing my fingers along her silky-smooth skin.

She won't let me distract her. She shakes her head, her hair rustling on the pillow. "No, that's not an answer. I know what you've done. I even know when."

"Is that so."

"After you went crazy and sent in that nurse to treat me…she gave me some kind of shot and knocked me out. You had a GPS tracker implanted in me while I was unconscious. That's how you found us in Ohio – you always knew where I was. From the minute I ran away."

She's a clever girl. "Maybe," I acknowledge.

"So why did you wait two months to come get me? All that talk about how much you needed me. Either you wanted me back or you didn't. It doesn't make sense."

I shift in the bed and sit up again, avoiding her gaze. I don't want to answer her, because it exposes a weakness, and I despise weakness. But she deserves the truth – as much as I can afford to give her, anyway.

"Because you terrify me, Willow. Since the day I lost Pyotr, I haven't let myself need anything or anyone. And then you came into my life, and when you aren't with me, your absence burns the thoughts from my brain. I hoped that with time, my desire for you would fade, but it got worse. Every single minute of every single day, I ached for you, until I couldn't take it anymore."

She manages a shaky laugh. "That's equal parts romantic and demented."

"An apt description of me, I imagine. Actually, that's giving myself too much credit in the romance part of the equation."

"So. The GPS tracker. Where in my body is it?"

"Doesn't matter."

She stiffens with resentment, turning her battered face towards me. "It's my body, so yes, it does matter. Take it out."

I bark a disbelieving laugh. "Hello, my name is Sergei. I *thought* you knew me, but apparently you don't know me at all. I don't take orders from anyone."

She lets out a sigh of exasperation. "All right, I will ask you nicely then. Please take your spy device out of my body. *Sir.*"

Oh, I missed hearing that. But I'm not going to budge.

I stare into her blue-gray eyes. "No. It's how I keep you safe."

"It's how you keep me under control!"

I shrug. "Does it matter why? It's not coming out."

Her gaze drops, and she shifts in bed, turning her back to me. This should be my signal to go, but I can't summon up the will to leave her. Not yet.

We lie in silence for several minutes, and I watch her chest rise and fall.

I think she's fallen asleep, but then she rolls over and looks at me again, her eyes drooping with exhaustion.

"I want you to know, when you punished me...I was a willing participant," she murmurs. "You like to hurt me. I like pain. I was horrified to realize that, and I tried to blame you for creating that perverse desire, but it's not your fault. It's just how I'm made. Pain gives me pleasure. I don't ever want you to feel bad about it."

I won't let myself off the hook that easily. Neither should she. "Hurting your flesh was all right, because I knew it was what you wanted and needed. Hurting your feelings wasn't."

"No, it wasn't," she agrees. "But I think we're better now. The two of us, together. I know you hate to hear me say nice things to you, but too bad. I forgive you for the things that you did, and I understand your motivation, even if you shouldn't have done it. And I appreciate everything that you did for my family. I don't think you even let yourself acknowledge how generous you are. You act like being decent is a character flaw, but it's not. All those things you've done for people, for no motive other than giving them what you knew they needed? It means that you didn't let my family corrode your soul. They lost. You won. You're still good."

That snatches my breath away, and I sit in stunned silence. Once upon a time, those words would have sent me into a burning rage, but that was before I met Willow. Now, I can let her stroke salve onto my wounded soul and not lash back.

How did she look into the toxic wasteland inside me, and see the bright shining threads of humanity still glowing? Only she could have done that. Nobody else.

I close my eyes, and realize that there are tears burning my lids.

"Thank you," I husk, floating in a sea of gratitude and sorrow. I don't dare move. Time passes as I drift in a bubble, weightless and without care.

"What happens now?" she asks me. And I crash back to earth, and it's every bit as painful as I imagined.

"We take it one day at a time," I say, and kiss her forehead.

But I'm lying. Because I'm filth. Lower than low.

I already know what's going to happen. Soon, I will have to do a terrible thing to her.

To the woman I love.

I admit that now. I've fallen in love with her. I need to leave now, to carry on my plan. I need to keep moving forward, through the pain and the self-hatred and the nuclear fallout I'll create with my final betrayal.

TWENTY-FOUR

Day twenty-nine...

Twenty-two hours since I've let myself see Willow. That shouldn't matter, but it does. I've checked in on her every day. I've told her that I can't be with her more often because I'm busy wrapping up an enormous project for work – the first time I've ever felt the need to explain my actions to her, or anyone.

It's 7:30 in the morning in California, 6:30 p.m. in the Pevlova Oblast.

The media room is our war room today. We sit there by the computer, taking phone calls, reading emails, watching video feeds. Coordinating with our men on the ground.

Yesterday we did something truly evil – even for us. We opened up the whorehouse that we'd spent the last couple of months building. It's in a tiny, remote town, an hour from the city of Pevlovagrad. Cataha recently rounded up a new shipment of girls. We hijacked his shipment and took them to our own brothel, and handed them over to the eager clients from all over the Pevlova oblast, the men who think their money and connections confer the right to rule over lesser mortals like cruel gods.

There was no other way to shut down the trafficking in the area for good. The mayor and the police chief of the central city of Pevlovagrad, both of whom were in power when my brother and I were taken fourteen years ago, were still in power, and still addicted to abusing women. They were also addicted to taking bribes from traffickers and wealthy clients in exchange for protection. As long as they were still in office, the trafficking business in Pevlova would never end.

So we let the men in our new whorehouse have their way with the women. Just one more black mark in my book of sins. We needed the men's crimes on video.

After a few hours, when we'd gotten enough video on the secret surveillance system that we'd installed in the building, we contacted Akim. If we'd just contacted the local police department, there wouldn't have been a raid at all. But with the media alerted, the police had no choice.

The police called ahead at the whorehouse to let the security detail know they were coming, so the place could be cleared out of girls and clients. But the security detail work for me, and so, oops, the warning never got passed along.

So the police swooped in and were angry to see that everyone was still there. Reluctantly, they rescued the women, and they made half a dozen token arrests of the least important men there, and they let the police chief and the mayor go.

But we had captured it all on video, and now we've struck our final blow. We've sent the video to Akim, and it's exploded. It's gone viral on social media. It's front-page news all over the world. The federal police storm in, and the mayor is dragged out of his house in front of the news cameras, in his pajamas, screaming and crying. The police chief knows what he can expect in prison; rather than submitting to a lifetime of being beaten and ass-raped, he opens fire on the men who have come to take him in, wounding several before they kill him. Much too merciful and fast an ending, but at least it is an ending.

Even better, it sends a message to the smaller police departments throughout the entire oblast, and the surrounding districts as well. They will be less likely to take bribes from traffickers, or even to allow the traffickers to operate in their districts, because now they fear suffering the same fate. When they are notified of trafficking operations, they'll be obligated to act, or risk exposure.

I could take this news to Willow to reassure her that she's right, that there is still some human decency in me.

But instead, I'm going to tell her something else. I'm going to twist it around. Make myself a villain. I'll tell her some lies, I'll tell her some truths.

It's the only way to save her.

She's the only thing that matters.

* * *

WILLOW

It's warm this afternoon, about eighty degrees, which is rare this far up the coast. The sun has burned away the last wisps of morning fog. I'm outside in the xeriscaped portion of the garden, strolling along pebbled paths among the cactuses and succulents.

I can't believe I've made it to thirty days this time.

I smile ruefully at the thought. Once upon a time, I couldn't wait for my captivity to be over. Now I can't wait to see what Sergei has planned for us next.

Anastasia hurries up the pebbled path, waving a fat sheaf of papers.

"It's all here!" she cries out.

"Say what, now?"

"The deed to this house. In your name." She grins at me, her eyes dancing with excitement.

Uneasiness prickles me.

Oblivious, she chatters away. "This house was purchased with legitimate money. He told me that he offered you the house, and you said you'd only take it if he could prove he didn't buy it with dirty money."

I shake my head in denial. That isn't exactly what I said. He offered me the house, and I said I wouldn't take anything purchased with dirty money. I didn't say I'd accept the house.

Anastasia continues. "I've read through all the paperwork, I made phone calls and went online to look at property records to verify it. He owned a chain of warehouses nationwide, and he sold that company to purchase this property. And now he's transferred it into your name."

"What? But I don't want it!" Full-blown panic is blooming inside me. This is bad. This is wrong.

"But why?" Anastasia's smooth brow wrinkles in confusion. "The money that Vilyat gave me? You were right, Willow. That money is filth, and it's wrong for me to keep it. I talked to Helenka and Yuri about it. We sent the money as a donation to Operation Salvat."

"You know what it is? We couldn't find it anywhere online. How did you find out?"

At that, her smile falters. "I called an old friend of mine in St. Petersburg, Raisa. She was one of the little girls from the whorehouse where I was taken. One of the few survivors. Poor girl was there getting screwed a hundred times a week until she was fifteen and managed to escape. She's scarred up inside, can't have kids. Now she's an anti-trafficking activist. Operation Salvat is a secret group that helps victims of human trafficking. They're kind of like a modern day underground railroad. They hide them, buy them new identities, give them money to buy a new start. So now Vilyat's filthy money is being given back to his victims. Poetic justice, yes?"

"Yes. I just…I don't feel right taking this house. Or Sergei's money."

Anastasia looks worried now. "Without it, we literally have nothing, Willow. The IRS are crawling all over Vilyat's finances. They're going to take every asset we ever had."

I make myself nod my head. "I see. Then…I guess we have to stay here. I mean, it does have those great rooms he set up for the kids… It's beautiful, it's safe here…"

If he's giving us the house, what does that mean for him and me?

She babbles on. "He's got a trust fund set up to pay the taxes and maintenance for this house, for the next thirty years. How wonderful is that? We can all live here. Helenka and Yuri and you and me. Nobody will be after us. We can live our lives. We can do whatever we want. Yuri is talking about designing cars. Helenka wants to open a chain of self-defense studios for women when she grows up. Isn't that glorious?"

I force myself to answer in a bright, cheerful tone.

"It's amazing! Really great! Wow, I…didn't expect that at all."

I am getting colder and colder. I can't feel the sunshine at all. I see Jasha heading towards us on the path. I don't like the look on his face.

Anastasia looks at me skeptically. "Willow? Why aren't you happy? This is a party! This is time to crack open the champagne! Are you feeling all right?"

"I don't know yet." No, I'm pretty sure I know. I'm pretty sure that soon, I won't be in a mood to celebrate.

"Hey, Jasha! Why the sour puss? We are all celebrating! Get us some champagne and come dance with me!" She does a little dance move, swaying her hips and grinning at him in a way I've never seen her smile at a man.

For her, he manages to crack a smile. "I will in a little while. We'll dance all night long, I promise."

"Woo-hoo!" she spins in a happy circle. "Willow, I'm going to cheer you up if it kills me."

Jasha gestures at me, and with a sinking heart, I hurry towards him, letting me lead me inside.

He takes me to Sergei's office. I've only been there once before.

He's on the phone as I come in. Waving his free arm around. For some reason, I notice that the braided bracelet that he always wore before is gone now. I've never seen him without it. The bracelet woven from the sinews of the wolf that killed his little brother.

He's shedding his past.

Sergei's voice booms through the air. "That's great, Ludmila. You're beautiful. Love you! I'll see you soon. I can't wait."

He hangs up and looks up at me as I stand there, swaying, in shock.

As if I'm so stupid that I wouldn't guess that he arranged for me to come in at just the right time, so I'd hear that phone call.

"Oh, hi, Willow. I just wanted to make sure that you got the paperwork. Everything's all arranged. I'll be leaving tonight."

I storm across the room. "What the hell was that?" I demand. "Who were you talking to?"

The words that he says are impossible words. They don't belong in his mouth. "My wife."

His wife?

I gasp. I stagger, and Jasha, who has hurried up next to me, catches me so I don't fall.

"You're lying."

He shakes his head.

"No. I warned you about me, Willow. How many times do I need to tell you what an utter bastard I am? But I do want to thank you You've served your purpose. You helped me find your uncle."

"This isn't you," I say desperately. "You said you cared about me."

He nods, and the pity on his face is a knife through my gut. "I do. I didn't lie about that. I meant every word I said. You are a wonderful woman. A man can care about more than one woman, can't he? But I have obligations. I need to get back to my real family."

Furious, I snatch a decorative inkwell from his desk and throw it at him, and it bounces off his forehead. Blood trickles down his face.

Jasha just stands there. He doesn't try to stop me, or to defend his boss.

"This isn't you, it's not, it's not!" I'm desperate for proof, something I can say that will make him stop stabbing me with hideous, brutal words. "You're not evil!" I scream at him. "You...you're running Operation Salvat! I know what it is, it's a rescue group! You help take down traffickers, you help save the victims!"

"No," he shakes his head. "Not at all. I need to keep track of them so they don't interfere with my own operations."

Is he trying to claim that he's a trafficker himself? That's madness. Why would he tell me such a sick lie?

Tears pour down my face, and I'm shaking with sobs. "Now I know you're lying. I know it! There are things even you can't fake.

You hate people who traffic in children. I've seen your physical reaction."

Sergei nods. Words march out of his mouth, strung together in sentences that must be, have to be, fiction.

"That's true. I would never traffic children. And really, we're not as bad as the other traffickers. All our girls are eighteen or older, and we actually pay them a percentage of the money they earn. They all get to use condoms and they're tested for disease every week. We don't bring in men who would torture or harm them. And after three years, we let them go, with enough money that they can start over in life. I mean, by the end of the three years, they don't look that good anymore anyway, so they're not worth as much."

Every single word is a knife blow. I cannot survive this.

I can't be that wrong.

He can't be a pimp.

"Stop lying to me!" I scream. I'm a desperate, panicked animal. "Why are you doing this?"

He just sits there without a word, and the sad sympathy gleaming from his eyes is worse than a punch to the face.

I grab a metal globe paperweight and throw it at him with all my strength, and it gashes him so hard that blood sprays from his cheek. Scarlet rivulets run down his face and splash onto his shirt.

He doesn't move at all.

I realize he'll just stand there and take anything I dish out at him. He won't stop me. Jasha won't stop me. I think Sergei would let me kill him. I almost think he'd welcome it.

But I can't.

"I love you. I want you to stay with me," I plead.

"You want to stay with a married man who's a pimp? You want to come to Russia with me and be my mistress?" He looks puzzled. Blood runs down his cheek and drips onto his shirt. "You know, you were right that Lukas is my son. My wife misses her son. My work is done here, and we need to go home."

"Fuck you! You lying bastard! If you want to break up with me, you could say so without lying like this."

"Exactly." He spreads his palms. He doesn't even try to staunch the steady river of blood that continues to flow. "I have no need to lie. Which should make it pretty obvious that I'm telling the truth."

"You are a coward! A disgusting, filthy, coward." Once upon a time, if I insulted him like that, he would have turned into a raging beast. He would have dragged me down the hall to his playroom and beaten me until my flesh burned with agonizing pleasure, and then he would have had sex with me. He would have made me beg for his tongue and his cock.

That will never happen again.

Because my world just flipped inside out into a horrible lunatic nightmare. The sun is cold and up is down and words are bullets.

I'm crying so hard now that I'm dizzy. I fall to my knees and wail. I hug myself, screaming and rocking.

Jasha kneels down next to me. He pats my back awkwardly.

"He shouldn't have done that to you," he says.

Shouldn't have done what? Lied, or told the truth?

Either one is the end of my world.

I plant my palms on the floor in a desperate attempt to hold myself steady. The room is spinning.

"Listen," Jasha's voice is saying from the ceiling. "My mission, my work for Sergei, is done. I will stay here with Anastasia and the children, and I will protect them. And you! Of course, you too. That is my new mission."

I've seen the way he looks at Anastasia. I've seen how the kids' mistrust of him has turned to admiration, how they follow him around pestering him with questions, and how he answers, gruffly but with affection. How protective he is, how he chides them when they do anything that he thinks might possibly put them in danger.

He will stay with them. They'll be all right. Thank God for that, because I'm falling into an abyss with no bottom.

I look up and Sergei is gone.

I try to stand, and fall back to my knees. My thirty days is up. Sergei was as good as his word. He didn't just set me free; he expelled me from his world.

Sergei left, and he took my heart with him.

I curl up in a tight ball, rocking, my mind splintering.

"This isn't over," I scream at the indifferent heavens, my voice crazed. I don't know what I'll do next, but I'm no longer sweet little Willow, the girl who bends for everyone. He doesn't get to do this to me. I will find out the whole truth of the man, no matter how ugly it is, no matter the consequences.

And if he's telling the truth, if he's married, and a human trafficker – then heaven help him, because I will tear his life to shreds like the monster I've become. Like the monster that he made me.

* * *

SERGEI

Day thirty, nighttime...

As my plane glides over the twinkling landscape below, I glare out of the window, and I don't bother to try to hide the tears streaming from my eyes. My men have never seen me like this before, but everything about our life is new and strange now. They pour themselves drinks from the minibar, and Maks shoves a bottle of vodka and a glass at me.

I open it without looking at it and drink directly from the bottle.

There are so many things that I want to tell her, need to tell her, and I can't.

An hour ago, Jasha gave me a look of utter disgust and fury when I went to say goodbye to him. His arm was looped around Anastasia's slender waist, and she clung to him and looked like she wanted to murder me. Our little group of survivors is shrinking. Now I've just got Maks and Slavik in my inner circle.

Slavik clears his throat. "It's not that I like her, or care about her. I mean, she's Vasily's daughter. And I've never questioned you before. But...you didn't need to do that."

My voice is raspy with sorrow. "I did. I broke her heart, but I saved her life."

"Let the stupid bitch cry until she chokes," Maks growls. "She's a fucking Toporov."

"Watch what you say about her." I clench my shaking fist.

"Yes, sir." His voice is thick with resentment. His gaze is dull. He's dazed by our success. He paces back and forth and doesn't seem to know what to do with himself.

"You don't need to come with me, you know. Either of you. Because this is a suicide mission we're on now."

"At least it's a mission." Maks flings himself back in his chair. He's reacting as I thought he might. Killing Vilyat and shutting down the last of the traffickers was a high. Now he's on a low. Without a mission, he'll fall apart. Earlier today, I offered him ownership of any of my companies, and he just cursed me and threw a cup of coffee at the wall.

As for Slavik, his face is impassive as usual, and I can't tell what he's feeling, but he also refused to take over any of my businesses, and he looked insulted when I suggested he didn't have to come with me.

The plane rises higher and higher, taking me away from my love, my life. I wish I could tell her why I've done what I've done. I wish I could take her with me, but that would be selfish, and if there's one thing that I've finally learned from Willow, it's that I need to do at least one selfless thing in my life, to be worthy of the love that she gave me.

The love that I'll never have again.

Thanks so much for buying
"THIRTY DAYS OF SHAME"!

If you'd like to be notified of future releases, freebies, contests and more, please sign up for my newsletter at
https://app.getresponse.com/site2/gingertalbot?u=B1VF6&webforms_id=AI0D

And remember, it's…NOT THE END!

Look out for "**THIRTY DAYS OF HATE**",
the thrilling conclusion to Willow and Sergei's story,
to be published the first week of
January 2018!

Printed in Great Britain
by Amazon